OTHER BOOKS BY
GRAHAM GREENE

NOVELS

The Man Within
Orient Express (Stamboul Train)*
It's a Battlefield
England Made Me (The Shipwrecked)*
This Gun for Hire (A Gun for Sale)*
Brighton Rock
The Confidential Agent
The Power and the Glory
The Ministry of Fear
The Heart of the Matter
The Third Man
The End of the Affair
Loser Takes All
The Quiet American
Our Man in Havana
A Burnt-Out Case
The Comedians
Travels with My Aunt
The Honorary Consul
The Human Factor
Dr. Fischer of Geneva, or The Bomb Party

MONSIGNOR QUIXOTE

GRAHAM GREENE

SIMON AND SCHUSTER
NEW YORK

Copyright © 1982 by Graham Greene
All rights reserved
including the right of reproduction
in whole or in part in any form
Published by Simon and Schuster
A Division of Gulf & Western Corporation
Simon & Schuster Building
Rockefeller Center
1230 Avenue of the Americas
New York, New York 10020
First published in Canada by Lester & Orpen Dennys Ltd.
SIMON AND SCHUSTER and colophon
are trademarks of Simon & Schuster
Designed by Edith Fowler
Manufactured in the United States of America

10 9 8 7 6 5 4 3 2 1

Library of Congress Cataloging in Publication Data

Greene, Graham, date.
  Monsignor Quixote.

  I. Title.
PR6013.R44M6 1982   821'.912   82-5937
ISBN 0-671-45818-3   AACR2

ACKNOWLEDGMENT

I acknowledge with gratitude my debt
to J. M. Cohen's translation
in the Penguin Classics
of Cervantes' *Don Quixote*.

G. G.

For Father Leopoldo Durán
Aurelio Verde
Octavio Victoria
        and
Miguel Fernández,
my companions on the roads of Spain,
and to Tom Burns, who inspired my
first visit there in 1946.

There is nothing either good or bad
but thinking makes it so.

—SHAKESPEARE

PART ONE

1
HOW FATHER QUIXOTE
BECAME A MONSIGNOR

It happened this way. Father Quixote had ordered his solitary lunch from his housekeeper and set off to buy wine at a local cooperative eight kilometers away from El Toboso on the main road to Valencia. It was a day when the heat stood and quivered on the dry fields, and there was no air-conditioning in his little Seat 600 which he had bought, already second hand, eight years before. As he drove he thought sadly of the day when he would have to find a new car. A dog's years can be multiplied by seven to equal a man's, and by that calculation his car would still be in early middle age, but he noticed how already his parishioners began to regard his Seat as almost senile. "You can't trust it, Don Quixote," they would warn him, and he could only reply, "It has been with me through many bad days, and I pray God that it may survive me." So many of his prayers had remained unanswered that he had hopes that this one prayer of his had lodged all the time like wax in the Eternal ear.

He could see where the main road lay by reason of the small dust puffs raised by the passing cars. As he drove he worried about the fate of his Seat, which he called in memory of his ancestor "my Rocinante." He couldn't bear the thought of his little car rusting in a scrap heap. He had sometimes thought of buying a small plot of land and leaving it as an inheritance to one of his parishioners on condition that a sheltered corner be reserved for his car to rest in, but there was not one parishioner whom he could trust to carry out his wish, and in any case a slow death by rust could not be avoided and perhaps a crusher at a scrapyard would be a more merciful end. Thinking of all this for the hundredth time he nearly ran into a stationary black Mercedes which was parked round the corner on the main road. He assumed that the dark-clothed figure at the wheel was taking a rest on the long drive from Valencia to Madrid, and he went on to buy his jar of wine at the collective without pausing; it was only as he returned that he became aware of a white Roman collar, like a handkerchief signaling distress. How on earth, he wondered, could one of his brother priests afford a Mercedes? But when he drew up he noticed a purple bib below the collar which denoted at least a monsignor if not a bishop.

Father Quixote had reason to be afraid of bishops; he was well aware of how much his own bishop, who regarded him in spite of his distinguished ancestry as little better than a peasant, disliked him. "How can he be descended from a fictional character?" he had demanded in a private conversation which had been promptly reported to Father Quixote.

The man to whom the bishop had spoken asked with surprise, "A *fictional* character?"

"A character in a novel by an overrated writer called Cervantes—a novel moreover with many disgusting passages which in the days of the Generalissimo would not even have passed the censor."

"But, Your Excellency, you can see the house of Dulcinea in El Toboso. There it is marked on a plaque: the house of Dulcinea."

"A trap for tourists. Why," the bishop went on with asperity, "Quixote is not even a Spanish patronymic. Cervantes himself says the surname was probably Quixada or Quesada or even Quexana, and on his deathbed Quixote calls himself Quixano."

"I can see that you have read the book then, Your Excellency."

"I have never got beyond the first chapter. Although of course I have glanced at the last. My usual habit with novels."

"Perhaps some ancestor of the father was called Quixada or Quexana."

"Men of that class have no ancestors."

It was with trepidation then that Father Quixote introduced himself to the high clerical figure in the distinguished Mercedes. "My name is Padre Quixote, monsignor. Can I be of any service?"

"You certainly can, my friend. I am the Bishop of Motopo"—he spoke with a strong Italian accent.

"Bishop of Motopo?"

"*In partibus infidelium*, my friend. Is there a garage near here? My car refuses to go on any farther, and if there should be a restaurant—my stomach begins to clamor for food."

"There is a garage in my village, but it is closed because of a funeral—the mother-in-law of the garagist has died."

"May she rest in peace," the bishop said automatically, clutching at his pectoral cross. He added, "What a confounded nuisance."

"He'll be back in a few hours."

"A few hours! Is there a restaurant anywhere near?"

"Monsignor, if you would honor me by sharing my humble lunch . . . the restaurant in El Toboso is not to be recommended, either for the food or for the wine."

"A glass of wine is essential in my situation."

17

"I can offer you a good little local wine and if you would be contented with a simple steak . . . and a salad. . . . My housekeeper always prepares more than I can eat."

"My friend, you certainly prove to be my guardian angel in disguise. Let us go."

The front seat of Father Quixote's car was occupied by the jar of wine, but the bishop insisted on crouching—he was a very tall man—in the back. "We cannot disturb the wine," he said.

"It is not an important wine, monsignor, and you will be much more comfortable . . ."

"No wine can be regarded as unimportant, my friend, since the marriage at Cana."

Father Quixote felt rebuked and silence fell between them until they arrived at his small house near the church. He was much relieved when the bishop, who had to stoop to enter the door which led directly into the priest's parlor, remarked, "It is an honor for me to be a guest in the house of Don Quixote."

"My bishop does not approve of the book."

"Holiness and literary appreciation don't always go together."

The bishop went to the bookshelf where Father Quixote kept his missal, his breviary, the New Testament, a few tattered volumes of a theological kind, the relics of his studies, and some works by his favorite saints.

"If you will excuse me, monsignor . . ."

Father Quixote went to find his housekeeper in the kitchen which served also as her bedroom, and it must be admitted the kitchen sink was her only washbasin. She was a square woman with protruding teeth and an embryo moustache; she trusted no one living, but had a certain regard for the saints, the female ones. Her name was Teresa, and nobody in El Toboso had thought to nickname her Dulcinea, since no one but the Mayor, who was reputed to be Communist, and the owner of the restaurant had read Cervantes' work, and it was doubtful if the latter had got much farther than the battle with the windmills.

"Teresa," Father Quixote said, "we have a guest for lunch, which must be prepared quickly."

"There is only your steak and a salad, and what remains of the Manchego cheese."

"My steak is always big enough for two, and the bishop is an amiable man."

"The bishop? I won't serve him."

"Not *our* bishop. An Italian. A very courteous man."

He explained the situation in which he had found the bishop.

"But the steak . . ." Teresa said.

"What about the steak?"

"You can't give the bishop horsemeat."

"My steak is horsemeat?"

"It always has been. How can I give you beef with the money you allow me?"

"You have nothing else?"

"Nothing."

"Oh dear, oh dear. We can only pray that he doesn't notice. After all, I have never noticed."

"*You* have never eaten anything better."

Father Quixote returned to the bishop in a troubled state of mind, carrying with him a half bottle of marsala. He was glad when the bishop accepted a glass and then a second one. Perhaps the drink might confuse his taste buds. He had settled himself deeply in Father Quixote's only easy chair. Father Quixote watched him with anxiety. The bishop didn't look dangerous. Father Quixote regretted that he had neglected to shave that morning after early Mass which he had celebrated in an empty church.

"You're on holiday, monsignor?"

"Not exactly on holiday, though it is true I am enjoying   19 my change from Rome. The Holy Father has entrusted me with a little confidential mission because of my knowledge of Spanish. I suppose, father, that you see a great many foreign tourists in El Toboso."

"Not many, monsignor, for there is very little for them to see here, except for the Museum."

"What do you keep in the Museum?"

"It is a very small museum, monsignor, one room. No bigger than my parlor. It holds nothing of interest except the signatures."

"What do you mean by 'the signatures'? May I perhaps have another glass of marsala? Sitting in the sun in that broken-down car has made me very thirsty."

"Forgive me, monsignor. You see how unused I am to being a host."

"I have never before encountered a Museum of Signatures."

"You see, a mayor of El Toboso years ago began writing to heads of state asking for translations of Cervantes with a signature. The collection is quite remarkable. Of course there is General Franco's signature in what I would call the master copy, and there is Mussolini's and Hitler's (very tiny, his, like a fly's mess) and Churchill's and Hindenburg's and someone called Ramsay MacDonald—I suppose he was the Prime Minister of Scotland."

"Of England, father."

Teresa came in with the steaks and they seated themselves at table and the bishop said grace.

Father Quixote poured out the wine and watched with apprehension as the bishop took his first slice of steak, which he quickly washed down with wine—perhaps to take away the taste.

"It is a very common wine, monsignor, but here we are very proud of what we call the Manchegan."

"The wine is agreeable," the bishop said, "but the steak
20   . . . the steak," he said, staring at his plate while Father

Quixote waited for the worst, "the steak . . ." he said a third time as though he were seeking deep in his memory of ancient rites for the correct term of anathema—Teresa meanwhile hovered in the doorway, waiting too—"never, at any table, have I tasted . . . so tender, so flavorsome, I am tempted to be blasphemous and say so divine a steak. I would like to congratulate your admirable housekeeper."

"She is here, monsignor."

"My dear lady, let me shake your hand." The bishop held out his beringed hand palm down as though he expected a kiss rather than a shake. Teresa backed hurriedly into the kitchen. "Did I say something wrong?" the bishop asked.

"No, no, monsignor. It is only that she is unaccustomed to cooking for a bishop."

"She has a plain and honest face. In these days one is often embarrassed to find even in Italy very *marriageable* housekeepers—and alas! only too often marriage does follow."

Teresa came rapidly in with some cheese and retired at the same speed.

"A little of our *queso manchego*, monsignor?"

"And perhaps another glass of wine to go with it?"

Father Quixote began to feel warm and comfortable. He was encouraged to press a question which he wouldn't have dared to ask his own bishop. A Roman bishop after all was closer to the fount of faith, and the bishop's welcome to the steak of horsemeat encouraged him. It was not for nothing that he had called his Seat 600 Rocinante, and he was more likely to receive a favorable answer if he spoke of her as a horse.

"Monsignor," he said, "there is one question I have often asked myself, a question which is perhaps likely to occur more frequently to a countryman than to a city dweller." He hesitated like a swimmer on a cold brink. "Would you consider it heretical to pray to God for the life of a horse?"

"For the terrestrial life," the bishop answered without

hesitation, "no—a prayer would be perfectly allowable. The fathers teach us that God created animals for man's use, and a long life of service for a horse is as desirable in the eyes of God as a long life for my Mercedes which, I am afraid, looks like failing me. I must admit, however, that there is no record of miracles in the case of inanimate objects, but in the case of beasts we have the example of Balaam's ass who by the mercy of God proved of more than usual use to Balaam."

"I was thinking less of the use of a horse to its master than a prayer for its happiness—and even for a good death."

"I see no objection to praying for its happiness—it might well make it docile and of greater use to its owner—but I am not sure what you mean by a good death in the case of a horse. A good death for a man means a death in communion with God, a promise of eternity. We may pray for the terrestrial life of a horse, but not for its eternal life—that would surely be verging on heresy. It is true there is a movement in the Church which would grant the possibility that a dog may have what one may call an embryo soul, though personally I find the idea sentimental and dangerous. We mustn't open unnecessary doors by imprudent speculation. If a dog has a soul, why not a rhinoceros or a kangaroo?"

"Or a mosquito?"

"Exactly. I can see, father, that you are on the right side."

"But I have never understood, monsignor, how a mosquito could have been created for man's use. What use?"

"Surely, father, the use is obvious. A mosquito may be likened to a scourge in the hands of God. It teaches us to endure pain for love of Him. That painful buzz in the ear —perhaps it is God buzzing."

Father Quixote had the unfortunate habit of a lonely

man: he spoke his thought aloud. "The same use would apply to a flea." The bishop eyed him closely, but there was no sign of humor in Father Quixote's gaze: it was obvious that he was plunged far in his own thoughts.

"These are great mysteries," the bishop told him. "Where would our faith be if there were no mysteries?"

"I am wondering," Father Quixote said, "where I have put the bottle of cognac that a man from Tomelloso brought me some three years back. This might be the right moment for opening it. If you will excuse me, monsignor. . . . Teresa may know." He made for the kitchen.

"He has drunk quite enough for a bishop," Teresa said.

"Hush! Your voice carries. The poor bishop is very worried about his car. He feels it has failed him."

"In my opinion, it is all his own fault. When I was a young girl I lived in Africa. Negroes and bishops always forget to refill with petrol."

"You really think . . . ? It's true he is a very unworldly man. He believes that the buzz of a mosquito. . . . Give me the cognac. While he drinks I'll see if I can do anything about his car."

He took a jerrycan of petrol from the boot of Rocinante. He didn't believe the problem was as simple as all that, but there was no harm in trying, and sure enough the tank was empty. Why hadn't the bishop noticed? Perhaps he had and was too ashamed to admit his foolishness to a country priest. He felt sorry for the bishop. Unlike his own bishop, the Italian was a kind man. He had drunk the young wine without complaint, he had eaten the horse steak with relish. Father Quixote didn't want to humiliate him. But how was he to save the bishop's face? He ruminated for a long time against the bonnet of the Mercedes. If the bishop had not noticed the gauge it would surely be easy to pretend a mechanical knowledge which he didn't possess. In any case it would be as well to get some oil on his hands. . . .

The bishop was quite happy with the cognac from Tomelloso. He had found on the shelves among the textbooks
a copy of Cervantes' work which Father Quixote had
bought when he was a boy, and he was smiling over a page
as Father Quixote's own bishop would certainly not have
done.

"Here is a very apposite passage, father, which I was
reading as you came in. What a moral writer Cervantes
was, whatever your bishop may say. 'It is a duty of loyal
vassals to tell their lords the truth in its proper shape and
essence without enlarging on it out of flattery or softening
it for any idle reason. I would have you know, Sancho, that
if the naked truth were to come to the ears of princes,
unclothed in flattery, this would be a different age.' In what
condition did you find the Mercedes, has it been bewitched
by some sorcerer in this dangerous region of La Mancha?"

"The Mercedes is ready to be driven, monsignor."

"A miracle? Or has the garagist returned from the funeral?"

"The garagist has not yet returned, so I took a look at the
engine myself." He held out his hands. "A messy job. You
were very low in petrol—that was easy to remedy, I always
have a spare jerrycan—but what was the real fault?"

"Ah, it wasn't only the petrol," the bishop said with sat-·
isfaction.

"There were some adjustments to be made to the engine
—I never know the technical names for these things—it
needed a good deal of fiddling around, but it is working satisfactorily now. Perhaps when you reach Madrid,
monsignor, it would be as well to get a professional over-
haul."

"Then I can be off?"

"Unless you would like to have a short siesta. Teresa
could prepare my bed."

"No, no, father. I feel completely refreshed by your excellent wine and the steak—ah, the steak. Besides, I have a dinner tonight in Madrid and I don't like driving in the dark."

As they made their way to the main road the bishop questioned Father Quixote. "For how many years have you lived in El Toboso, father?"

"Since my childhood, monsignor. Except during my studies for the priesthood."

"Where did you study?"

"In Madrid. I would have preferred Salamanca, but the standard there was beyond me."

"A man of your ability is wasted in El Toboso. Surely your bishop. . . ."

"My bishop, alas, knows how small my abilities are."

"Could your bishop have mended my car?"

"My spiritual abilities, I meant."

"In the Church we have need of men of practical abilities too. In the world of today *astucia*—in the sense of worldly wisdom—must be allied to prayer. A priest who can set before an unexpected guest good wine, good cheese and a remarkable steak is a priest who can hold his own in the highest circles. We are here to bring sinners to repentance and there are more sinners among the bourgeois than among peasants. I would like you to go forth like your ancestor Don Quixote on the high roads of the world. . . ."

"He was a madman, monsignor."

"So many said of Saint Ignatius. But here is one high road I have to take and here is my Mercedes. . . ."

"He was a fiction, my bishop says, in the mind of a writer. . . ."

"Perhaps we are all fictions, father, in the mind of God."

"Do you want me to tilt at windmills?"

"It was only by tilting at windmills that Don Quixote found the truth on his deathbed," and the bishop, seating himself at the wheel of the Mercedes, intoned in Gregorian accents, " 'There are no birds this year in last year's nests.' "

"It's a beautiful phrase," Father Quixote said, "but what did he mean by it?"

"I have never quite made it out myself," the bishop replied, "but surely the beauty is enough," and as the Mercedes purred with gentle health on the road towards Madrid, Father Quixote realized with his nose that the bishop had left behind him for a brief instant an agreeable smell compounded of young wine, of cognac, and of Manchegan cheese which before it dispersed a stranger might well have mistaken for an exotic incense.

Many weeks passed with all the comforting unbroken rhythms of former years. Now that Father Quixote knew that his occasional steak consisted of horsemeat he would greet it with an unguilty smile—no need to reproach himself for luxury—in memory of the Italian bishop who had shown such kindness, such courtesy, such love of wine. It seemed to him that one of the pagan gods he had read about in his Latin studies had rested for an hour or two under his rooftree. He read very little now except his breviary and the newspaper, which had never informed him that the breviary was no longer required reading; he was interested particularly in the accounts of the cosmonauts since he had never quite been able to abandon the idea that somewhere in the immensity of space existed the realm of God—and occasionally he would open one of his old theological textbooks to make sure that the short homily which he would be making in the church on Sunday was properly in accordance with the teaching of the Church.

He also received once a month from Madrid a theological magazine. There were criticisms in it referring sometimes to dangerous ideas—spoken even by a cardinal, in Holland or Belgium, he forgot which—or written by a priest who had a Teutonic name which put Father Quixote in mind of

Luther—but he paid little attention to such criticisms, for it was very unlikely that he would have to defend the ortho-doxy of the Church against the butcher, the baker, the garagist or even the restaurant keeper who was the most educated man in El Toboso except for the Mayor, and as the Mayor was believed by the bishop to be an atheist and a Communist, he could safely be ignored as far as the doc-trine of the Church was concerned. Indeed, Father Qui-xote enjoyed the Mayor's company for a street-corner chat more than that of his parishioners. In the company of the Mayor, he ceased to feel himself a kind of official superior; they had the equality of a common interest in the progress through space of the cosmonauts, and they were tactful with each other. Father Quixote did not speak of the pos-sibility of an encounter between a sputnik and the angelic host and the Mayor showed a scientific impartiality be-tween the Russian and the American achievements—not that Father Quixote saw much difference between the crews from a Christian point of view—both crews seemed to him to consist of good people, probably good parents and good husbands, but in their helmets and space suits, which might well have been provided by the same haberdasher, he couldn't imagine either of them in the company of Ga-briel or Michael, and certainly not of Lucifer if instead of rising to the realm of God their spaceship should take a headlong spin towards the infernal regions.

"You've got a letter," Teresa told him with suspicion. "I didn't know where to find you."

"I was up the street talking to the Mayor."

"That heretic."

"If there were no heretics, Teresa, there would be little for a priest to do."

She snarled at him, "It's a letter from the bishop."

"Oh dear, oh dear." He sat with it for a long time in his hand, fearing to open it. He couldn't remember a single letter from his bishop which hadn't included a complaint of one kind or another. There had been, for example, the time when he had diverted the Easter offering which traditionally belonged in his own pocket to the pocket of a representative of a charity with the worthy Latin name of In Vinculis, purporting to look after the spiritual needs of poor imprisoned men. It was a private act of benevolence which had somehow reached the bishop's ears after the collector had been arrested for organizing the escape of certain incarcerated enemies of the Generalissimo. The bishop had called him a fool—a term which Christ had deprecated. The Mayor on the other hand had clapped him on the back and called him a worthy descendant of his great ancestor who had released the galley slaves. And then there was the time . . . and that other time . . . he would have given himself a glass of marsala to give him courage had there been any left after he had entertained the Bishop of Motopo.

With a sigh he broke the red seal and opened the envelope. As he had feared, the letter seemed to have been written in a cold rage. "I have received an utterly incomprehensible letter from Rome," the bishop wrote, "which at first I took for a joke in the worst of taste, imitating an ecclesiastical style and possibly inspired by a member of that Communist organization which you thought it your duty to support from motives which have always been obscure to me. But on asking for confirmation I have today received an abrupt letter confirming the first missive and asking me at once to communicate to you that the Holy Father has seen fit—for what strange stirring of the Holy Spirit it is not for me to enquire—to promote you to the rank of Monsignor, apparently on the recommendation of a Bishop of Motopo, of whom I have never heard, without any reference to me through whom such a recommendation should naturally have come—a most unlikely action on my part, I need hardly add. I have obeyed the Holy Father in passing on the news to you, and I can only pray that you will not disgrace the title he has seen fit to grant you. Certain scandals which were only forgiven because they originated in the ignorance of the parish priest of El Toboso would have far greater resonance if caused by the imprudence of Monsignor Quixote. So prudence, my dear father, prudence, I beg of you. I have written to Rome, however, pointing out the absurdity of a small parish like El Toboso being in the hands of a Monsignor, a title which will be resented by many deserving priests in La Mancha, and asking for aid in finding a wider scope for your activities, perhaps in another diocese or even in the mission field."

He closed the letter and it dropped to the floor. "What does he say?" Teresa asked.

"He wants to drive me away from El Toboso," Father Quixote said in a tone of such despair that Teresa went quickly back into the kitchen to hide from his sad eyes.

II

HOW MONSIGNOR QUIXOTE
SET OFF
ON HIS TRAVELS

1

It happened a week after the bishop's letter had been de-
livered to Father Quixote that local elections were held in
the province of La Mancha and the Mayor of El Toboso
suffered an unexpected defeat. "The forces of the Right,"
he told Father Quixote, "have re-formed, they seek another
Generalissimo," and he spoke of certain intrigues of which
he was very well informed between the garagist, the
butcher, and the owner of the second-rate restaurant, who,
it seemed, wanted to enlarge his premises. Money, he said,
had been lent to the landlord by a mysterious stranger and
as a result he had bought a new deep freeze. In some way
which Father Quixote was quite unable to fathom, this had
seriously affected the election results.

"I wash my hands of El Toboso," the ex-Mayor said.

"And I am being driven away by the bishop," Father
Quixote confided, and he told his melancholy story.

"I could have warned you. This comes of putting your
trust in the Church."

"It is not a question of the Church but of a bishop. I have
never cared for the bishop, may God forgive me. But you,
that is another matter. I am deeply sorry for you, my dear
friend. You have been let down by your party, Sancho."

The Mayor's name was Zancas, which was the surname of the original Sancho Panza in Cervantes' truthful history, and though his Christian name was Enrique he permitted his friend Father Quixote to tease him with the name of Sancho.

"It is not a question of my party. Three men alone have done this to me," and he mentioned again the butcher, the garagist, and the affair of the deep freeze. "There are traitors in every party. In your party too, Father Quixote. There was Judas. . . ."

"And in yours there was Stalin."

"Don't bring up that old stale history now."

"The history of Judas is even older."

"Alexander the Sixth. . . ."

"Trotsky. Though I suppose you may be allowed now to have a difference of opinion about Trotsky." There was little logic in their argument, but it was the nearest they had ever come to a quarrel.

"And what about your opinion of Judas? He's a saint in the Ethiopian Church."

"Sancho, Sancho, we disagree too profoundly to dispute. Let us go to my house and have a glass of marsala. . . . Oh, I forgot, the bishop finished the bottle."

"The bishop. . . . You allowed that scoundrel. . . ."

"It was a different bishop. A good man, but the cause of my trouble all the same."

"You had better come to my house then and have a glass of honest vodka."

"Vodka?"

"Polish vodka, father. From a Catholic country."

It was the first time Father Quixote had tasted vodka. The first glass seemed to him to lack flavor—the second gave him a sense of exhilaration. He said, "You will miss your duties as a mayor, Sancho."

"I plan to take a holiday. I have not stepped out of El

Toboso since the death of that scoundrel Franco. If only I had a car. . . ."

Father Quixote thought of Rocinante and his mind wandered.

"Moscow is too far," the voice of the Mayor went on. "Besides it is too cold. East Germany . . . I have no desire to go there, we have seen too many Germans in Spain."

Suppose, Father Quixote thought, I am expelled to Rome. Rocinante could never make so great a distance. The bishop had even spoken of a mission field. Rocinante was near the end of her days. He couldn't leave her to die by some roadside in Africa to be cannibalized for the sake of a gearbox or a door handle.

"San Marino is the nearest state where the Party rules. Another glass, father?"

Without thinking Father Quixote extended his hand.

"What will you do, father, away from El Toboso?"

"I shall obey orders. I will go where I am sent."

"To preach to the converted as you do here?"

"That is an easy sneer, Sancho. I doubt if anyone is ever fully converted."

"Not even the Pope?"

"Perhaps, poor man, not even the Pope. Who knows what he thinks at night in his bed when he has said his prayers?"

"And you?"

"Oh, I am as ignorant as anyone in the parish. I have read more books, that is all, when I was studying, but one forgets. . . ."

"All the same you do believe all that nonsense. God, the Trinity, the Immaculate Conception. . . ."

"I *want* to believe. And I want others to believe."

"Why?"

"I want them to be happy."

"Let them drink a little vodka then. That's better than a make-believe."

"The vodka wears off. It's wearing off even now."

"So does belief."

Father Quixote looked up with surprise. He had been gazing with a certain wistfulness at the last drops in his glass.

"Your belief?"

"And your belief."

"Why do you think that?"

"It's life, father, at its dirty work. Belief dies away like desire for a woman. I doubt if you are an exception to the general rule."

"Do you think it would be bad for me to have another glass?"

"Vodka has never done anyone any harm."

"I was astonished the other day at how much the Bishop of Motopo drank."

"Where is Motopo?"

"*In partibus infidelium.*"

"I've long ago forgotten the little Latin I once had."

"I didn't know you ever had any."

"My parents wanted me to be a priest. I even studied at Salamanca. I have never told you that before, father. *In vodka veritas.*"

"So that was how you knew about the Ethiopian Church? I was a little surprised."

"There are small bits of useless knowledge which stick to one's brain like barnacles to a boat. By the way, you have read how the Soviet cosmonauts have beaten the endurance record in outer space?"

"I heard something of the sort on the radio yesterday."

"Yet in all that time they haven't encountered a single angel."

"Have you read, Sancho, about the black holes in space?"

"I know what you are going to say, father. But the word 'holes' is used only in a metaphoric sense. One more glass. Don't be afraid of any bishop."

33

"Your vodka inspires me with hope."

"Of what?"

"A forlorn hope you would say."

"Go on. Tell me. What hope?"

"I can't tell you. You would laugh at me. One day perhaps I will tell you of my hope. If God grant me the time. And you the time too, of course."

"We should see more of each other, father. Perhaps I will convert you to Marx."

"You have a Marx on your shelves?"

"Of course."

"*Das Kapital?*"

"Yes. Among others. There it is. I haven't read any of it for a long time. To tell you the truth I've always found parts . . . well, remote . . . all the statistics about the English industrial revolution. I imagine you find parts of the Bible dull too."

"Thank God, we are not expected to study Numbers or Deuteronomy, but the Gospels are not dull. My goodness, look at the time. Is it vodka that makes time go so fast?"

"You know, father, you remind me of your ancestor. He believed in all those books of chivalry, quite out of date even in his day. . . ."

"I've never read a book of chivalry in my life."

"But you continue to read those old books of theology. They are your books of chivalry. You believe in them just as much as he did in his books."

"But the voice of the Church doesn't date, Sancho."

"Oh yes, father, it does. Your second Vatican Council put even Saint John out of date."

"What nonsense you talk."

"No longer at the end of Mass do you read those words of Saint John—'He was in the world and the world was made by Him and the world knew Him not.' "

"How strange you should know that."

"Oh, I've sometimes come in at the end of Mass—to make sure none of my people are there."

"I still say those words."

"But you don't say them aloud. Your bishop wouldn't allow it. You are like your ancestor who read his books of chivalry secretly so that only his niece and his doctor knew until—"

"What a lot of nonsense you talk, Sancho."

"—until he broke away on Rocinante to do his deeds of chivalry in a world that didn't believe in those old stories."

"Accompanied by an ignorant man called Sancho," Father Quixote replied with a touch of anger which he immediately regretted.

"Accompanied by Sancho," the Mayor repeated. "Why not?"

"The bishop could hardly deny me a short holiday."

"You must go to Madrid to buy your uniform."

"Uniform? What uniform?"

"Purple socks, monsignor, and a purple—what do you call that thing they wear below the collar?"

"A *pechera*. That's rubbish. Nobody will make me wear purple socks and a purple. . . ."

"You're in the army of the Church, father. You can't refuse the badges of rank."

"I never asked to be a monsignor."

"Of course you could retire from the army altogether."

"Could you retire from the Party?"

Each took another glass of vodka and fell into a comradely silence, a silence in which their dreams had room to grow.

"Do you think your car could get us as far as Moscow?"

"Rocinante is too old for that. She'd break down on the way. Anyway the bishop would hardly consider Moscow a suitable place for me to take a holiday."

"You are no longer the bishop's servant, monsignor." 35

"But the Holy Father. . . . You know, Rocinante might perhaps get as far as Rome."

"I don't fancy Rome at all. Nothing to be seen in the streets but purple socks."

"Rome has a Communist mayor, Sancho."

"I don't fancy a Euro-Communist any more than you fancy a Protestant. What's the matter, father? You are upset about something."

"The vodka gave me a dream, and another vodka has taken it away."

"Don't worry. You aren't used to vodka and it has gone to your head."

"Why such a happy dream . . . and afterwards despair?"

"I know what you mean. Vodka sometimes has that effect on me, if I take a little too much. I'll see you home, father."

At Father Quixote's door they parted.

"Go and lie down for a while."

"Teresa would find it rather odd at this hour. And I haven't yet read my breviary."

"That's no longer compulsory, surely? "

"I find it hard to break a habit. Habits can be comforting, even rather boring habits."

"Yes. I think I understand. There are even times when I dip into *The Communist Manifesto*."

"Does it comfort you?"

"Sometimes—a little, not very much. But a little."

"You must lend it to me. One day."

"Perhaps on our travels."

"You still believe in our travels? I doubt very much whether we are the right companions, you and I. A big gulf separates us, Sancho."

"A big gulf separated your ancestor from the one you call mine, father, and yet. . . ."

"Yes. And yet. . . ." Father Quixote turned hurriedly away. He went into his study and took his breviary from the shelf, but before reading more than a few sentences he fell asleep, and all that he could remember after he had woken was that he had been climbing a high tree and he had dislodged a nest, empty and dry and brittle, the relic of a year gone by.

2

It needed a great deal of courage for Father Quixote to write to the bishop and an even greater courage to open the letter which in due course he received in reply. The letter began abruptly, "Monsignor"—and the sound of the title was like acid on the tongue. "El Toboso," the bishop wrote, "is one of the smallest parishes in my diocese, and I cannot believe that the burden of your duties has been a very heavy one. However, I am ready to grant your request for a period of repose and I am dispatching a young priest, Father Herrera, to look after El Toboso in your absence. I trust that at least you will delay your holiday until you are fully satisfied that Father Herrera is aware of all the problems which may exist in your parish, so you can leave your people with complete confidence in his care. The defeat of the Mayor of El Toboso in the recent election seems to indicate that the tide is turning at last in the proper direction and perhaps a young priest with the shrewdness and discretion of Father Herrera (he won golden opinions as well as a doctorate in moral theology at Salamanca) will be better able to take advantage of the current than an older man. As you will guess I have written to the Archbishop with regard to your future, and I have small doubt that by the time you return from your holiday we will have found you a sphere of action more suitable than El Toboso and carrying a lesser burden of duties for a priest of your age and rank."

It was an even worse letter than Father Quixote had expected, and he waited with growing anxiety for the arrival of Father Herrera. He told Teresa that Father Herrera should take immediate possession of his bedroom and asked her to find, if it were possible, a folding camp bed for the living room. "If you cannot find one," he said, "the armchair is quite comfortable enough for me. I have slept in it often enough in the afternoon."

"If he's young let him sleep in the armchair."

"For the time being he is my guest, Teresa."

"What do you mean—for the time being?"

"I think that the bishop is likely to make him my successor in El Toboso. I am getting old, Teresa."

"If you are that old you shouldn't go galavanting off—the good God alone knows where. Anyway, don't expect me to work for another priest."

"Give him a chance, Teresa, give him a chance. But don't on any account tell him the secret of your admirable steaks."

Three days passed and Father Herrera arrived. Father Quixote, who had gone to have a chat with the ex-Mayor, found the young priest on the doorstep carrying a smart black suitcase. Teresa was barring his entrance, a kitchen cloth in her hand. Father Herrera was perhaps naturally pale, but he looked agitated, and the sun gleamed on his clerical collar. "Monsignor Quixote?" he asked. "I am Father Herrera. This woman won't let me in."

"Teresa, Teresa, this is very unkind of you. Where are your manners? This is our guest. Go and get Father Herrera a cup of coffee."

"No. Please not. I never drink coffee. It keeps me awake at night."

In the sitting room Father Herrera took the only armchair without hesitation. "What a very violent woman," he said. "I told her that I was sent by the bishop and she said something very rude."

"Like all of us, she has her prejudices."

"The bishop would *not* have been pleased."

"Well, he didn't hear her, and we won't tell him, will we?"

"I was quite shocked, monsignor."

"I wish you wouldn't call me monsignor. Call me father if you like. I'm old enough to be your father. Have you experience of parish work?"

"Not directly. I've been His Excellency's secretary for three years. Since I left Salamanca."

"You may find it difficult at first. There are many Teresas in El Toboso. But I am sure you will learn very quickly. Your doctorate was in . . . let me remember."

"Moral theology."

"Ah, I always found that a very difficult subject. I very nearly failed to pass—even in Madrid."

"I see you have Father Heribert Jone on your shelf. A German. All the same, very sound on that subject."

"I am afraid I haven't read him for many years. Moral theology, as you can imagine, doesn't play a great part in parish work."

"I would have thought it essential. In the confessional."

"When the baker comes to me, or the garagist—it's not very often—their problems are usually very simple ones. Well, I trust to my instinct. I have no time to look their problems up in Jone."

"Instinct must have a sound basis, monsignor—I'm sorry —father."

"Oh yes, of course, a sound basis. Yes. But like my ancestor, perhaps I put my trust most in old books written before Jone was born."

"But your ancestor's books were only ones of chivalry, surely?"

"Well, perhaps mine—in their way—are of chivalry too. Saint John of the Cross, Saint Teresa, Saint Francis de Sales. And the Gospels, father. 'Let us go up to Jerusalem and die with Him.' Don Quixote could not have put it better than Saint Thomas."

"Oh, of course, one accepts the Gospels, naturally," Father Herrera said in the tone of one who surrenders a small and unimportant point to his adversary. "All the same, Jone on moral theology is very sound, very sound. What's that you said, father?"

"Oh, nothing. A truism which I haven't the right to use. I was going to add that another sound base is God's love."

"Of course, of course. But we mustn't forget His justice either. You agree, monsignor?"

"Yes, well, yes, I suppose so."

"Jone makes a very clear distinction between love and justice."

"Did you take a secretarial course, father? After Salamanca, I mean."

"Certainly. I can type and without boasting I can claim to be very good at shorthand."

Teresa put her head round the door. "Will you have a steak for lunch, father?"

"Two steaks, please, Teresa."

The sunlight flashed again on Father Herrera's collar as he turned: the flash was like a helio signal sending what message? Father Quixote thought he had never before seen so clean a collar or indeed so clean a man. You would have thought, so smooth and white was his skin, that it had never required a razor. That comes from living so long in El Toboso, he told himself, I am a rough countryman. I live very, very far away from Salamanca.

3

The day of departure came at last. Rocinante had been
passed by the garagist, though rather grudgingly, as fit to

leave. "I can guarantee nothing," he said. "You should have turned her in five years ago. All the same she ought to get you as far as Madrid."

"And back again, I hope," Father Quixote said.

"That is another matter."

The Mayor could hardly contain his impatience to be gone. He had no desire to see his successor installed. "A black Fascist, father. We shall soon be back in the days of Franco."

"God rest his soul," Father Quixote added with a certain automatism.

"He had no soul. If such a thing exists."

Their luggage filled the boot of Rocinante and the back seat was given up to four cases of honest Manchegan wine. "You can't trust the wine in Madrid," the Mayor said. "Thanks to me we have at least an honest cooperative here."

"Why should we go to Madrid?" Father Quixote asked. "I remember I disliked the city a great deal when I was a student and I have never been back. Why not take the road to Cuenca? Cuenca, I am told, is a beautiful town and a great deal nearer to El Toboso. I don't want to overtire Rocinante."

"I doubt if you can buy purple socks in Cuenca."

"Those purple socks! I refuse to buy purple socks. I can't afford to waste money on purple socks, Sancho."

"Your ancestor had a proper respect for the uniform of a knight errant, even though he had to put up with a barber's basin for a helmet. You are a monsignor errant and you must wear purple socks."

"They say my ancestor was mad. They will say the same of me. I will be brought back in disgrace. Indeed I must be a little mad, for I am mocked with the title of monsignor and I am leaving El Toboso in charge of that young priest."

41

"The baker has a poor opinion of him and I've seen him myself in close talk with that reactionary of the restaurant."

Father Quixote insisted on taking the wheel. "Rocinante has certain tricks of her own which only I know."

"You are taking the wrong road."

"I have to go to the house once more. I have forgotten something."

He left the Mayor in the car. The young priest, he knew, was at the church. He wanted to be alone for the last time in the house where he had lived for more than thirty years. Besides, he had forgotten Father Heribert Jone's work on moral theology. Saint John of the Cross was in the boot and so were Saint Teresa and Saint Francis de Sales. He had promised Father Herrera, though a little unwillingly, to balance these old books with a more modern work of theology which he had not opened since the days when he was a student. "Instinct must have a sound basis in belief," Father Herrera had correctly said. If the Mayor began to quote Marx to him Father Heribert Jone might perhaps prove useful in reply. Anyway it was a small book which fitted easily into a pocket. He sat down for a few moments in his armchair. The seat had been shaped by his body through the years and its shape was as familiar to him as the curve of the saddle must have been to his ancestor. He could hear Teresa move pans in the kitchen, keeping up the angry mutter which had been the music of his morning solitude. I will miss even her ill humor, he thought. Outside the Mayor impatiently sounded the horn.

"I'm sorry to have kept you waiting," Father Quixote said, and Rocinante gave a deep groan as he changed gear.

They said very little to each other. It was as though the strangeness of their adventure weighed on their spirits. Once the Mayor spoke his thought aloud. "We must have something in common, father, or why do you go with me?"

42   "I suppose—friendship?"

"Is that enough?"

"We will find out in time."

More than an hour passed in silence. Then the Mayor spoke again. "What is upsetting you, friend?"

"We have just left La Mancha and nothing seems safe any more."

"Not even your faith?"

It was a question which Father Quixote did not bother to answer.

III

HOW A CERTAIN LIGHT
WAS SHED UPON
THE HOLY TRINITY

The distance from El Toboso to Madrid is not very great, but what with the faltering gait of Rocinante and the queue of lorries which stretched ahead the evening found Father Quixote and the Mayor still on the road.

"I am hungry and thirsty," the Mayor complained.

"And Rocinante is very tired," Father Quixote replied.

"If only we could find an inn, but the wine along the main road is not to be trusted."

"We have plenty of good Manchegan with us."

"But food. I must have food."

"Teresa insisted on putting a parcel on the back seat. She told me it was in case of an emergency. She had no more trust, I'm afraid, in poor Rocinante than the garagist."

"But this *is* an emergency," the Mayor said.

Father Quixote opened the parcel. "Praise be to God," he said, "a big Manchego cheese, some smoked sausages, even two glasses and two knives."

"I don't know about praise to God, but certainly praise to Teresa."

"Oh well. It is probably the same thing, Sancho. All our good actions are acts of God, just as all our ill actions are acts of the Devil."

44

"In that case you must forgive our poor Stalin," the Mayor said, "for perhaps only the Devil was responsible."

They drove very slowly, looking out for a tree that would give them shade, for the late sun was slanting low across the fields, driving the shadows into patches far too thin for two men to sit in them at ease. Finally, under the ruined wall of an outhouse which belonged to an abandoned farm, they found what they needed. Someone had painted a hammer and sickle crudely in red upon the crumbling stone.

"I would have preferred a cross," Father Quixote said, "to eat under."

"What does it matter? The taste of the cheese will not be affected by cross or hammer. Besides is there much difference between the two? They are both protests against injustice."

"But the results were a little different. One created tyranny, the other charity."

"Tyranny? Charity? What about the Inquisition and our great patriot Torquemada?"

"Fewer suffered from Torquemada than from Stalin."

"Are you quite sure of that—relative to the population of Russia in Stalin's day and of Spain in Torquemada's?"

"I am no statistician, Sancho. Open a bottle—if you have a corkscrew."

"I am never without one. But you have the knives. Skin me a sausage, father."

"Torquemada at least thought he was leading his victims towards eternal happiness."

"And Stalin too perhaps. It is best to leave motives alone, father. Motives in men's minds are a mystery. This wine would have been much better chilled. If only we could have found a stream. Tomorrow we must buy a thermos as well as your purple socks."

"If we are to judge simply by actions, Sancho, then we must look at results."

"A few million dead and Communism is established over nearly half the world. A small price. One loses more in any war."

"A few hundred dead and Spain remains a Catholic country. An even smaller price."

"So Franco succeeds Torquemada."

"And Brezhnev succeeds Stalin."

"Well, father, we can at least agree with this: that small men seem always to succeed the great, and perhaps the small men are easier to live with."

"I'm glad you recognize greatness in Torquemada."

They laughed and drank and were happy under the broken wall while the sun sank and the shadows lengthened, until without noticing it they sat in darkness and the heat came mainly from within.

"Do you really hope, father, that Catholicism one day will lead men to a happy future?"

"Oh yes, of course. I *hope*."

"Only after death though?"

"Do you hope that Communism—I mean the real Communism your prophet Marx spoke about—will ever arrive, even in Russia?"

"Yes, father. I hope, I do hope. But it's true—I only tell you because your lips are sealed as a priest and mine are opened by the wine—I do sometimes despair."

"Oh, despair I understand. I know despair too, Sancho. Not final despair, of course."

"Mine isn't final either, father. Or I wouldn't be sitting here on the ground beside you."

"Where would you be?"

"I would be buried in unconsecrated ground. Like other suicides."

"Let us drink to hope then," Father Quixote said and
46 raised his glass. They drank.

It is strange how quickly a bottle can be emptied when one debates without rancor. The Mayor poured the last few drops upon the ground. "For the gods," he said. "Mind you, I say the gods, not God. The gods drink deep, but your solitary God is, I'm sure, a teetotaller."

"You are saying what you know to be wrong, Sancho. You studied at Salamanca. You know very well that God, or so I believe, and perhaps you once believed, becomes wine every morning and every evening in the Mass."

"Well then, let us drink more and more of the wine your God approved of. At least this Manchegan is better than altar wine. Where did I put the corkscrew?"

"You are sitting on it. And don't talk so scornfully of altar wine. I don't know what Father Herrera will buy, but I use a perfectly good Manchegan. Of course, if the Pope is going to allow Communion in both kinds, I will have to buy something cheaper, but I trust he will consider the poverty of the priesthood. The baker has a great thirst. He would lap up a whole chalice."

"Let us raise another glass, father. To hope again."

"To hope, Sancho." And they clinked their glasses. The night was beginning to turn from cool to cold, but the wine still warmed them, and Father Quixote had no desire to hasten towards the city he disliked and to breathe the fumes of the lorries which continued to pass along the road in a chain of headlights.

"Your glass is empty, father."

"Thank you. A drop more. You are a good fellow, Sancho. I seem to remember that our two ancestors lay down for the night under the trees more than once. There are no trees here. But there is a castle wall. In the morning we will demand entrance, but now. . . . Give me a little more of the cheese."

"I am happy to be lying under the great symbol of the hammer and the sickle."

"The poor sickle has been rather neglected in Russia, don't you think, or they wouldn't have to buy so much wheat from the Americans?"

"A temporary shortage, father. We cannot yet control the climate."

"But God can."

"Do you really believe that?"

"Yes."

"Ah, you indulge too much, father, in a dangerous drug —as dangerous as the old Don's books of chivalry."

"What drug?"

"Opium."

"Oh, I understand. . . . That old saying of your prophet Marx—'Religion is the opium of the people.' But you take it out of context, Sancho. Just as our heretics have twisted the words of Our Lord."

"I don't follow you, monsignor."

"When I was a student in Madrid I was encouraged to read a little in *your* holy book. One must know one's enemy. Don't you remember how Marx defended the monastic orders in England and condemned Henry the Eighth?"

"I certainly do not."

"You should look at *Das Kapital* again. There is no talk of opium there."

"All the same, he wrote it—though I forget for a moment where."

"Yes, but he wrote it in the nineteenth century, Sancho. Opium then was not an evil drug—laudanum was a tranquilizer, nothing worse. A tranquilizer for the well-to-do, one which the poor could not afford. Religion is the Valium of the poor—that was all he meant. Better for them than a visit to a gin palace. Better for them perhaps even than this wine. Man can't live without a tranquilizer."

"Then perhaps we should kill another bottle?"

"Say half a bottle if we are to arrive safely in Madrid. Too much opium might be dangerous."

"We will make a Marxist of you yet, monsignor."

"I have packed some half bottles to fill up the corners."

The Mayor went to the car and returned with a half bottle.

"I have never denied that Marx was a good man," Father Quixote said. "He wanted to help the poor, and that want of his will certainly have saved him at the last."

"Your glass, monsignor."

"I have asked you not to call me monsignor."

"Then why not call me comrade—I prefer it to Sancho."

"In recent history, Sancho, too many comrades have been killed by comrades. I don't mind calling you friend. Friends are less apt to kill each other."

"Isn't friend going a little bit far between a Catholic priest and a Marxist?"

"You said a few hours back that we must have something in common."

"Perhaps what we have in common is this Manchegan wine, friend."

They both had a sense of growing comfort as the dark deepened and they teased each other. When the lorries passed on the road the headlights gleamed narrowly for a moment on the two empty bottles and what remained in the half bottle.

"What puzzles me, friend, is how you can believe in so many incompatible ideas. For example, the Trinity. It's worse than higher mathematics. Can you explain the Trinity to me? It was more than they could do in Salamanca."

"I can try."

"Try then."

"You see these bottles?"

"Of course."

"Two bottles equal in size. The wine they contained was   49 of the same substance and it was born at the same time. There you have God the Father and God the Son and there, in the half bottle, God the Holy Ghost. Same substance. Same birth. They're inseparable. Whoever partakes of one partakes of all three."

"I was never, even in Salamanca, able to see the point of the Holy Ghost. He has always seemed to me a bit redundant."

"We were not satisfied with two bottles, were we? That half bottle gave us the extra spark of life we both needed. We wouldn't have been so happy without it. Perhaps we wouldn't have had the courage to continue our journey. Even our friendship might have ceased without the Holy Spirit."

"You are very ingenious, friend. I begin at least to understand what *you* mean by the Trinity. Not to believe in it, mind you. That I will never do."

Father Quixote sat in silence looking at the bottles. When the Mayor struck a match to light a cigarette he saw the bowed head of his companion. It was as though he had been deserted by the Spirit he had praised. "What is the matter, father?" he asked.

"May God forgive me," Father Quixote said, "for I have sinned."

"It was only a joke, father. Surely your God can understand a joke."

"I have been guilty of heresy," Father Quixote replied. "I think—perhaps—I am unworthy to be a priest."

"What have you done?"

"I have given wrong instruction. The Holy Ghost is equal in all respect to the Father and the Son, and I have represented Him by this half bottle."

"Is that a serious error, father?"

"It is anathema. It was condemned expressly at I forget which Council. A very early Council. Perhaps it was Ni-
caea."

"Don't worry, father. The matter is easily put right. We will throw away and forget this half bottle and I will bring a whole bottle from the car."

"I have drunk more than I should. If I hadn't drunk so much I would never, never have made that mistake. There is no sin worse than the sin against the Holy Ghost."

"Forget it. We will put the matter right at once."

So it was they drank another bottle. Father Quixote felt comforted and he was touched too by the sympathy of his companion. The Manchegan wine was light, but it seemed wiser to them both to stretch out on the grass and sleep the night away where they were, and when the sun rose Father Quixote was able to smile at the sadness he had felt. There was no sin in a little forgetfulness and an inadvertent error. The Manchegan wine had been the guilty party—it was not, after all, quite so light a wine as he had believed.

As they set off he said, "I was a little foolish last night, Sancho."

"I thought you spoke very well."

"I did make you understand, perhaps, a little about the Trinity?"

"Understand, yes. Believe, no."

"Then will you please forget the half bottle? It was a mistake that I should never have made."

"I will remember only the full three bottles, friend."

IV

HOW SANCHO
IN HIS TURN
CAST NEW LIGHT
ON AN OLD FAITH

1

Perhaps, light though the wine had been, it was the three and a half bottles which made them next day travel for a while in silence. At last Sancho remarked, "We shall feel better after a good lunch."

"Ah, poor Teresa," Father Quixote said. "I hope Father Herrera will appreciate her steaks."

"What is so wonderful about her steaks?"

Father Quixote made no reply. He had guarded the secret from the Bishop of Motopo; he would certainly guard her secret from the Mayor.

The road curved. For an inexplicable reason Rocinante put on a spurt of speed instead of slowing down and nearly bumped into a sheep. The road ahead was full of its companions. They were like a disturbed sea of small frothing waves.

"You may as well sleep a bit more," the Mayor said. "We shall never get through this." A dog came charging back to round up the delinquent. "Sheep are stupid beasts," the Mayor exclaimed with venom. "I have never understood why the founder of your faith should have compared them with ourselves. 'Feed my sheep.' Oh yes, perhaps after all like other good men he was a cynic. 'Feed them well, make them fat, so that they can be eaten in their turn.' 'The Lord is my shepherd.' But if we are sheep why in heaven's name should we trust our shepherd? He's going to guard us from wolves all right, oh yes, but only so that he can sell us later to the butcher."

Father Quixote took the breviary from his pocket and began ostentatiously to read, but he had fallen on a singularly dull and unmeaning passage which quite failed to exclude the words of the Mayor, words which pained him.

"And he actually preferred sheep to goats," the Mayor said. "What a silly sentimental preference that is. The goat has all the uses that a sheep has and in addition many of the virtues of a cow. The sheep gives wool all right—but the goat gives its skin in man's service. The sheep provides mutton, but personally I would rather eat kid. And the goat, like the cow, provides milk and cheese. A sheep's cheese is fit only for Frenchmen."

Father Quixote raised his eyes and saw the way was clear at last. He put away his breviary and started Rocinante on the road again. "The man without faith cannot blaspheme," he said, as much to himself as to the Mayor. But he thought: all the same, why sheep? Why did He in His infinite wisdom choose the symbol of sheep? It was not a question that had been answered by any of the old theologians whom he kept on the shelves in El Toboso: not even by Saint Francis de Sales, informative as he was about the elephant and the kestrel, the spider and the bee and the partridge. Certainly the question had not been raised in the *Catecismo de la Doctrina Cristiana* by that holy man Antonio Claret, a former Archbishop of Santiago de Cuba, which he had read as a child—though he seemed to remember that a shepherd and his lambs had figured among the illustrations. He said irrelevantly, "Children have a great love for lambs."

"And goats," the Mayor said. "Don't you remember the

little goat carts of our childhood? Where are all those goats now? Condemned to the eternal flames?" He looked at his watch. "I suggest that before we buy your purple socks we give ourselves a good lunch at Botin's."

"I hope it's not a very expensive restaurant, Sancho."

"Don't worry. On this occasion you're my guest. The sucking-pigs are famous there—we won't have to eat any of the good shepherd's lambs, which are such a favorite in our country. Botin's was a restaurant very much favored by the secret police in the days of Franco."

"God rest his soul," Father Quixote said quickly.

"I wish I believed in damnation," the Mayor replied, "for I would certainly put him—as I am sure Dante would have done—in the lowest depths."

"I suspect human judgment, even Dante's," Father Quixote said. "It's not the same as the judgment of God."

"I expect you would put him in Paradise?"

"I've never said that, Sancho. I don't deny that he did many wrong things."

"Ah, but there's that convenient escape you've invented —Purgatory."

"I've invented nothing—neither Hell nor Purgatory."

"Forgive me, father. I meant of course your Church."

"The Church depends on written authority as your party depends on Marx and Lenin."

"But you believe your books are the word of God."

"Be fair, Sancho. Do you not think—except sometimes at night when you can't sleep—that Marx and Lenin are as infallible as—well, Matthew and Mark?"

"And when *you* can't sleep, monsignor?"

"The idea of Hell has sometimes disturbed my sleeplessness. Perhaps that same night in your room you are thinking of Stalin and the camps. Was Stalin—or Lenin— necessarily right? Perhaps you are asking that question at the same moment when I am asking myself whether it is possible . . . how can a merciful and loving God . . . ? Oh, I cling to my old books, but I have my doubts too. The other night—because of something Teresa said to me in the kitchen about the heat of her stove—I reread all the Gospels. Do you know that Saint Matthew mentions Hell fifteen times in fifty-two pages of my Bible and Saint John not once? Saint Mark twice in thirty-one pages and Saint Luke three times in fifty-two. Well, of course, Saint Matthew was a tax collector, poor man, and he probably believed in the efficacy of punishment, but it made me wonder. . . ."

"And how right you were."

"I hope—friend—that you sometimes doubt too. It's human to doubt."

"I try not to doubt," the Mayor said.

"Oh, so do I. So do I. In that we are certainly alike."

The Mayor put his hand for a moment on Father Quixote's shoulder, and Father Quixote could feel the electricity of affection in the touch. It's odd, he thought, as he steered Rocinante with undue caution round a curve, how sharing a sense of doubt can bring men together perhaps even more than sharing a faith. The believer will fight another believer over a shade of difference; the doubter fights only with himself.

"The thought of the sucking-pig at Botin's," the Mayor said, "reminds me of that pretty fable of the Prodigal Son. Of course I realize the difference, for in that story I think it was a calf the father slaughtered—yes, a fatted calf. I hope our sucking-pig will be as well fattened."

"A very beautiful parable," Father Quixote said with a note of defiance. He felt uneasy about what was to come.

"Yes, it begins beautifully," said the Mayor. "There is this very bourgeois household, a father and two sons. One might describe the father as a rich Russian kulak who regards his peasants as so many souls whom he owns."

"There is nothing about kulaks or souls in the parable."

"The story you have read has been probably a little corrected and slanted here and there by the ecclesiastical censors."

"What do you mean?"

"It could have been told so differently, and perhaps it was. Here is this young man who by some beneficent trick of heredity has grown up against all odds with a hatred of inherited wealth. Perhaps Christ had Job in mind. Christ was nearer in time to the author of Job than you are to your great ancestor, the Don. Job, you remember, was obscenely rich. He owned seven thousand sheep and three thousand camels. The son feels stifled by his bourgeois surroundings—perhaps even by the kind of furniture and the kind of pictures on the walls, of fat kulaks sitting down to their Sabbath meal, a sad contrast with the poverty he sees around him. He has to escape—anywhere. So he demands his share of the inheritance which will come to his brother and himself on their father's death and he leaves home."

"And squanders his inheritance in riotous living," Father Quixote interrupted.

"Ah, that is the official version. My version is that he was so disgusted by the bourgeois world in which he had been brought up that he got rid of his wealth in the quickest way possible—perhaps he even gave it away and in a Tolstoyan gesture he became a peasant."

"But he came home."

"Yes, his courage failed him. He felt very alone on that pig farm. There was no branch of the Party to which he could look for help. *Das Kapital* had not yet been written, so he was unable to situate himself in the class struggle. Is it any wonder that he wavered for a time, poor boy?"

"Only for a time? How do you make that out?"

"The story in your version is cut short rather abruptly, isn't it? By the ecclesiastical censors undoubtedly, even perhaps by Matthew, the tax collector. Oh, he is welcomed home, that's true enough, a fatted calf is served, he is probably happy for a few days, but then he feels again the same oppressive atmosphere of bourgeois materialism that drove him from home. His father tries to express his love, but the furniture is still hideous, false Louis Quinze or whatever was the equivalent in those days, the same pictures of good living on the walls, he is shocked more than ever by the servility of the servants and the luxury of the food, and he begins to remember the companionship he had found in the poverty of the pig farm."

"I thought you said there was no Party branch and that he felt very alone."

"Yes, I exaggerated. He did have one friend, and he remembered the words of this old bearded peasant who had helped him carry the swill to the pigs, he began to brood on them—the words I mean, not the pigs—back in the luxurious bed in which his bones yearned for the hard earth of his hut on the farm. After all, three thousand camels might well be enough to revolt a sensitive man."

"You have a wonderful imagination, Sancho, even when you are sober. What on earth did the old peasant say?"

"He told him that every state in which private ownership of the land and means of production exists, in which capital dominates, however democratic it may claim to be, is a capitalist state, a machine invented and used by the capitalists to keep the working class in subjection."

"Your story begins to sound almost as dull as my breviary."

"Dull? Do you call that dull? I'm quoting Lenin himself. Don't you see that the first idea of the class struggle is being lodged by that old peasant (I see him with a beard and whiskers like Karl Marx's) in the mind of the Prodigal Son?"

"And what does he do?"

"After a week of disillusion he leaves home at dawn (a

red dawn) to find again the pig farm and the old bearded peasant, determined now to play his part in the proletarian struggle. The old bearded peasant sees him coming from a distance and, running up, he throws his arms around his neck and kisses him, and the Prodigal Son says, 'Father, I have sinned, I am not worthy to be called your son.' "

"The ending sounds familiar," Father Quixote said. "And I'm glad you left in the pigs."

"Talking of pigs, couldn't you drive a little faster? I don't think we are averaging more than thirty kilometers an hour."

"That's Rocinante's favorite speed. She's a very old car and I can't make her strain—not at her age."

"We are being passed by every car on the road."

"What does it matter? Her ancestor never got up to thirty kilometers an hour."

"And your ancestor never got further in his travels than Barcelona."

"What of it? He remained almost in hailing distance of La Mancha, but his mind traveled very far. And so did Sancho's."

"I don't know about my mind, but my belly feels as though we had been a week on the road. The sausages and the cheese are a distant memory now."

It was a little after two when they mounted the stairs to Botin's. Sancho gave the order for two portions of sucking-pig and a bottle of the Marqués de Murrieta's red wine. "I'm surprised that you favor the aristocracy," Father Quixote remarked.

"They can be temporarily accepted for the good of the Party, like a priest."

"Even a priest?"

"Yes. A certain indisputable authority who shall be nameless"—he gave a hasty glance to the tables on either side—"wrote that atheist propaganda in certain circumstances may be both unnecessary and harmful."

"Was it really Lenin who wrote that?"

"Yes, yes, of course, but better not use that name here, father. One never knows. I told you the kind of people who used to come here in the days of our lamented leader. A leopard doesn't change his spots."

"Then why did you bring me here?"

"Because it's the best place for sucking-pig. Anyway, your collar makes you a partial protection. You will be even more so when you've got your purple socks and your purple. . . ."

He was interrupted by the sucking-pig—indeed for a while there was no opportunity to speak except by signs, which could hardly have been misinterpreted by any secret policeman: for example, the raising of a fork in honor of the Marqués de Murrieta.

The Mayor gave a sigh of satisfaction. "Have you ever eaten a better sucking-pig?"

"I have never before eaten a sucking-pig," Father Quixote replied with a certain sense of shame.

"What do you eat at home?"

"Usually a steak—I've told you Teresa is very good with steaks."

"The butcher is a reactionary and a dishonest man."

"His horse steaks are excellent." The forbidden word had slipped out before he could stop it.

2

Perhaps it was only the wine which gave Father Quixote the worldly strength to resist the Mayor. The Mayor wished to take rooms in the Palace Hotel and to pay for them himself, but one sight of the glittering, crowded hall was enough for Father Quixote. "How can you, a Communist . . . ?"

"The Party has never forbidden us to take advantage of   59 bourgeois comfort so long as it lasts. And surely here if anywhere we can best study our enemies. Besides, this hotel is nothing, I believe, compared with the new hotel in Moscow which they have built in the Red Square. Communism is not against comfort, even what you might call luxury, so long as the worker benefits in the long run. However, if you wish to be uncomfortable and mortify yourself. . . ."

"On the contrary. I am quite ready to be comfortable, but I wouldn't feel comfortable here. Comfort is a state of mind."

They drove into a poorer quarter of the city, taking streets at random. Suddenly Rocinante stopped and nothing would make her start again. There was the sign of an *albergue* twenty yards down the street, and a dingy doorway. "Rocinante knows best," Father Quixote said. "This is where we stay."

"But it's not even clean," the Mayor said.

"These are obviously very poor people. So I'm sure they will make us welcome. They need us. They didn't need us at the Palace Hotel."

An old woman greeted them in a narrow passage, with an air of incredulity. Although they saw no sign of other customers she told them that only one room was available, but it had two beds.

"Is there at least a bath?"

No, not exactly a bath, she told them, but there was a douche on the floor above and a basin with a cold-water tap in the room they would share. "We'll take it," Father Quixote said.

"You are mad," the Mayor told him when they were alone in the room, which Father Quixote admitted was rather gloomy. "We come to Madrid where there are dozens of good and inexpensive hotels, and you land us in this unspeakable hostelry."

"Rocinante was tired."

"We shall be lucky if our throats aren't cut here."

"No, no, the old woman is honest, I know."

"How do you know?"

"I could tell from her eyes."

The Mayor raised his hands in despair.

"After all that good wine," Father Quixote said, "we shall sleep well wherever we are."

"I shan't sleep a wink."

"She is one of your people."

"What on earth do you mean?"

"The poor." He added quickly, "Of course they are my people too."

Father Quixote felt much relieved when the Mayor lay down on his bed fully clothed (he feared that his throat would be cut more easily if he undressed), for Father Quixote was not used to taking off his clothes in front of another, and anything, anything, he thought, might happen before nightfall to save him from embarrassment. He lay on his back and listened to a cat wailing on the tiles outside. Perhaps, he thought, the Mayor will have forgotten my purple socks, and he indulged himself in a waking dream of how their journey would go on and on—the dream of a deepening friendship and a profounder understanding, of a reconciliation even between their disparate faiths. Perhaps, he thought before he fell asleep, the Mayor was not altogether wrong about the Prodigal Son . . . all that happy ending, the welcome home, the fatted calf. The close of the parable did seem a little unlikely. . . . "I am unworthy to be called your monsignor," he muttered as he lost consciousness.

It was the Mayor who woke him. Father Quixote saw him, like a stranger, in the last light of the expiring day, and "Who are you?" he asked with curiosity, not fear.

"I am Sancho," the Mayor said. "It is time for us to go shopping."

"Shopping?"

"You have become a knight. We must find your sword, your spurs, your helmet—even if it is only a barber's basin."

"Barber's basin?"

"You have been asleep and I have lain awake for three hours in case they tried to cut our throats. Tonight it will be your turn to keep vigil. In this dirty chapel that you've landed us in. Over your sword, monsignor."

"Monsignor?"

"You have certainly slept very deep."

"I've had a dream—a terrible dream."

"Of your throat being cut?"

"No, no. Much worse than that."

"Come. Get up. We have to find your purple socks."

Father Quixote made no protest. He was still under the agonizing spell of his dream. They went down the dark stairs into the dark street. The old woman peered out at them as they passed, with an appearance of terror. Had she been dreaming too?

"I don't like the look of her," Sancho said.

"I don't think she likes the look of us."

"We must find a taxi," the Mayor said.

"First let us try Rocinante."

He only had to press the starter three times before the engine woke. "You see," Father Quixote said, "there was nothing really wrong. She was just tired, that's all. I know Rocinante. Where do we go?"

"I don't know. I thought you would know."

"Know what?"

"An ecclesiastical tailor."

"How should I know?"

"You are a priest. You are wearing a priest's suit. You didn't buy that in El Toboso."

"It's nearly forty years old, Sancho."

"If you and your socks last as long as that you will be more than a centenarian before you wear them out."

"Why have I to buy these socks?"

"The roads in Spain are still controlled, father. Stuck in El Toboso you haven't realized how all along the roads of Spain the ghost of Franco still patrols. Your socks will be our safeguard. A Guardia Civil respects purple socks."

"But where do we buy them?" He brought Rocinante to a halt. "I'm not going to tire her for nothing."

"Stay here a moment. I will find a taxi and ask the driver to guide us."

"We are being very extravagant, Sancho. Why, you even wanted to stay at the Palace Hotel."

"Money is not an immediate problem."

"El Toboso is a small place, and I've never heard that mayors are paid very much."

"El Toboso is a small place, but the Party is a great party. What is more, the Party is a legal party now. As a militant one is allowed a certain license—for the good of the Party."

"Then why do you need the protection of my socks?"

But the question came too late. The Mayor was already out of earshot, and Father Quixote was alone with the nightmare that haunted him. There are dreams of which we think even in the light of day: was this a dream or was it true—true in some way or another? did I dream it or did it in some strange way happen?

The Mayor was opening the door beside him. He said, "Follow the taxi. He assures me he will lead us to the finest ecclesiastical clothes shop outside Rome itself. The Nuncio goes there and the Archbishop."

When they arrived Father Quixote could well believe it. His heart sank as he took in the elegance of the shop and the dark well-pressed suit of the assistant who greeted them with the distant courtesy of a church authority. It occurred to Father Quixote that such a man was almost certainly a 63 member of Opus Dei—that club of intellectual Catholic activists whom he could not fault and yet whom he could not trust. He was a countryman, and they belonged to the great cities.

"The monsignor," the Mayor said, "wants some purple socks."

"Of course, monsignor. If you will come this way."

"I wanted to see," the Mayor whispered as they followed, "if he would demand any papers."

Rather as though he were a deacon arranging the altar before Mass the assistant laid out on a counter a variety of purple socks. "These are nylon," he said. "These pure silk. And these are cotton. The best Sea Island cotton, of course."

"I usually wear wool," Father Quixote said.

"Oh well, of course we *have* wool, but we usually find nylon or silk preferred. It's a question of tone—silk or nylon has a richer purple tone. Wool rather blurs the purple."

"For me it's a question of warmth," Father Quixote said.

"I agree with this gentleman, monsignor," the Mayor interrupted quickly. "We want a purple which strikes the eye, as it were, from a distance."

The assistant looked puzzled. "From a distance?" he asked. "I don't quite. . . ."

"We don't want the purple to look accidental. We certainly don't want a non-ecclesiastical purple."

"No one has ever found fault with our purple. Even the woolen purple," the assistant added with reluctance.

"For our purpose," the Mayor said, giving a warning frown at Father Quixote, "the nylon is much the best. It certainly has a shimmer. . . ." He added, "And then, of course, we shall want . . . what do you call that sort of bib monsignors wear?"

"I suppose you mean the *pechera*. I imagine you will need that in nylon too so as to match the socks."

"I have agreed about the socks," Father Quixote said, "but I absolutely refuse to wear a purple *pechera*."

"Only in emergency, monsignor," the Mayor argued.

The assistant looked at them with deepening suspicion.

"I can't see what emergency. . . ."

"I've explained that to you—the state of the roads these days. . . ."

While the assistant did up the package which he closed carefully with a Scotch tape of the same ecclesiastical purple as the socks and the *pechera*, the Mayor, who had obviously taken a dislike to the man, began a needling conversation. "I suppose," he said, "you supply pretty well everything the Church needs—in the way of decoration."

"If you mean vestments, well, yes."

"And hats—birettas and the like?"

"Of course."

"And cardinals' hats? The monsignor has not reached that stage yet, of course. I'm just asking for interest. . . . One must be prepared. . . ."

"Cardinals' hats are *always* received from His Holiness."

Rocinante had one of her moods and took a little time to start. "I'm afraid I went too far," the Mayor said, "and aroused suspicion."

"What do you mean?"

"That man came to the door. I think he took the number of the car."

"I don't want to be unkind," Father Quixote said, "but he looked the kind of man who might belong to Opus Dei."

"They probably own the shop."

"Of course I'm sure they do a lot of good in their own way. Like the Generalissimo did."

"I would like to believe in Hell if only to put the members of Opus Dei there with the Generalissimo."

"He has my prayers," Father Quixote said and stiffened his fingers round the wheel of Rocinante.

"He'll need more than your prayers if there's a Hell."

"Since there is a Hell it will need only the prayers of one just man to save any of us. Like Sodom and Gomorrah," Father Quixote added, with some uncertainty whether he had got the statistics right.

It was a very hot evening. The Mayor suggested that they should have dinner at the Poncio Pilato, but Father Quixote was firm in his refusal. He said, "Pontius Pilate was an evil man. The world has almost canonized him because he was a neutral, but one cannot be neutral when it comes to choosing between good and evil."

"He was not neutral," the Mayor retorted. "He was non-aligned—like Fidel Castro—with a slant in the right direction."

"What do you mean by the right direction?"

"The Roman Empire."

"You—a Communist—support the Roman Empire?"

"Marx tells us that to arrive at the possibility of developing a revolutionary proletariat we have to pass through the stage of capitalism. The Roman Empire was developing into a capitalist society. The Jews were held back by their religion from ever becoming industrialists, so. . . ."

The Mayor then suggested that they eat at the Horno de Santa Teresa: "I don't know about her oven, but she was a saint very much admired by your friend the Generalissimo." Father Quixote could see no reason why food and religion had to be linked together, and he was irritated when the Mayor then proposed the San Antonio de la Florida, a saint of whom Father Quixote had no knowledge. He suspected the Mayor of teasing him. In the end they ate a rather bad meal at Los Porches where the open air made up a little for the deficiencies of the menu.

They killed one bottle of wine while they waited and a second with their meal, but when the Mayor suggested that they complete the Holy Trinity, Father Quixote refused.

He said he was tired, the siesta had done him no good, but these were excuses—it was really his dream that weighed on him. He longed to communicate it, although Sancho would never understand the distress it had caused him. If only he had been at home . . . and yet what difference would that have made? Teresa would have said, "It was only a dream, father," and Father Herrera. . . . It was an odd thing, but he knew that he could never communicate with Father Herrera on anything which touched the religion they were supposed to share. Father Herrera was in favor of the new Mass, and one evening at the end of a rather silent dinner Father Quixote had been unwise enough to tell him how at the end of Mass he had the habit of silently speaking the words of Saint John's Gospel which had been removed from the liturgy.

"Ah, poetry," Father Herrera had replied with a note of disapproval.

"You don't like Saint John?"

"The Gospel which goes by his name is not one of my favorites. I prefer Saint Matthew."

Father Quixote had found himself in a reckless mood that evening and he felt sure that an account of their conversation would be sent next day to the bishop. Alas! Too late. A monsignor can only be demoted by the Pope himself. He had answered, "I have always thought that the Gospel of Saint Matthew could be distinguished from the others as the Gospel of fear."

"Why? What an extraordinary idea, monsignor."

"In Saint Matthew there are fifteen references to Hell."

"What of it?"

"To govern by fear . . . surely God can leave that to Stalin or Hitler. I believe in the virtue of courage. I don't believe in the virtue of cowardice."

"A child has to be educated through discipline. And we are all children, monsignor."

"I don't think a loving parent would educate by fear."

"I hope this is not what you teach your parishioners."

"Oh, I don't teach them. They teach me."

"Hell is not the monopoly of Saint Matthew, monsignor. Do you feel the same about the other Gospels?"

"There's quite a big difference." Father Quixote hesitated, for he realized that now he was really on dangerous ground.

"What difference?" Perhaps Father Herrera was hoping for a truly heretical reply which could be reported—of course by the proper channels—to Rome.

Father Quixote told Father Herrera what he had told the Mayor. "In Saint Mark there are only two references to Hell. (Of course he had his own specialty—he was the Apostle of pity.) In Saint Luke three references—he is the great storyteller. From him come most of the great parables. And Saint John—they say now that it's the oldest Gospel of all, older than Saint Mark. It's very strange. . . ." He hesitated.

"Well, what about Saint John?"

"There's not one reference to Hell in his Gospel."

"But surely, monsignor, you are not questioning the existence of Hell?"

"I believe from obedience, but not with the heart."

Like a full stop it was the end of the conversation.

Father Quixote put on the brake in their dark and dreary street.

"The sooner we leave here the better," the Mayor said. "To think that we could have slept comfortably at the Palace."

A door opened as they passed up the stairs and the candlelight from an inner room showed the suspicious and scared face of the old woman.

"Why on earth does she look so frightened?" the Mayor asked.

"Perhaps our fear is catching," Father Quixote said. As quickly as possible he slipped underneath the sheets half undressed, but the Mayor took his time. He was more careful in folding his trousers and his jacket than Father Quixote, but he kept on his shirt and his underpants as though he too was prepared for some emergency.

"What on earth do you have in your pocket?" he asked, shifting Father Quixote's jacket.

"Oh, that's Jone on moral theology. I put it in my pocket at the last moment."

"What a book to bring on a holiday!"

"Well, I saw you had put a book of Lenin's essays in the car, and something by Marx."

"I thought I would lend them to you for your instruction."

"Well, I'll lend you Jone, if you like, for yours."

"It might at least send me to sleep," the Mayor said and extracted the small green book from Father Quixote's pocket.

Father Quixote lay on his back and listened to his companion turning the pages. Once the Mayor gave a yap of laughter. Father Quixote could remember nothing funny in Jone, but then it was forty years since he had read his *Moral Theology*. Sleep continued to escape him, while the terrible dream of his siesta stayed with him like a cheap tune in the head.

He had dreamt that Christ had been saved from the Cross by the legion of angels to which on an earlier occasion the Devil had told Him that He could appeal. So there was no final agony, no heavy stone which had to be rolled away, no discovery of an empty tomb. Father Quixote stood there watching on Golgotha as Christ stepped down from the Cross triumphant and acclaimed. The Roman soldiers, even the Centurion, knelt in His honor, and the people of Jerusalem poured up the hill to worship Him.   69

The disciples clustered happily around. His mother smiled through her tears of joy. There was no ambiguity, no room for doubt and no room for faith at all. The whole world knew with certainty that Christ was the Son of God.

It was only a dream, of course it was only a dream, but nonetheless Father Quixote had felt on waking the chill of despair felt by a man who realizes suddenly that he has taken up a profession which is of use to no one, who must continue to live in a kind of Saharan desert without doubt or faith, where everyone is certain that the same belief is true. He had found himself whispering, "God save me from such a belief." Then he heard the Mayor turn restlessly on the bed beside him, and he added without thought, "Save him too from belief," and only then he fell asleep again.

3

The old woman was waiting for them at the bottom of the stairs. There was a crack in the wood on the bottom step and Father Quixote stumbled and nearly fell. The old woman crossed herself and began to gabble at him, waving a piece of paper.

"What does she want?" the Mayor asked.

"Our name and address and where we've come from and where we are going."

"That's not a hotel *ficha*. It's just a piece of paper out of a notebook."

The gabble continued, rising in tone and threatening to become a scream.

"I can't understand a word," the Mayor said.

"You don't have the practice of listening which I have in the confessional. She says she's been in trouble before now with the police for not having a record of her guests. Communists they were, she says, and they were wanted men."

"Why didn't she make us do it when we arrived?"

"She thought we wouldn't take the room and then she forgot. Lend me a pen. It's not worth a fuss."

"One guest is enough. Especially when he's a priest. And don't forget to put in 'monsignor.' "

"Where shall I say we are going?"

"Write 'Barcelona.' "

"You never said anything about Barcelona."

"Who knows? We might go there. Your ancestor did. Anyway I have never believed in confiding anything personal to the police."

Father Quixote reluctantly obeyed. Would Father Jone have taken this for a lie? He remembered that Father Jone had divided lies rather oddly into malicious, officious, and jocose lies. This lie wasn't malicious, and it certainly wasn't jocose. Officious lies are told for one's own or another's advantage. He saw no advantage to anyone in a misstatement. Perhaps it wasn't a lie at all. It was even possible that their wanderings might one day take them to Barcelona.

V

HOW MONSIGNOR QUIXOTE
AND SANCHO
VISIT A HOLY SITE

Y ou want to go north?" Father Quixote asked. "I thought perhaps we might at least take a little turn in the direction of Barcelona."

"I am guiding you," the Mayor said, "to such a holy site that I feel sure you will want to say your prayers there. Follow the road towards Salamanca until I tell you when to turn off."

Something in the way he spoke gave Father Quixote cause for uneasiness. He fell silent and his dream came back to him. He said, "Sancho, do you really believe that one day all the world will be Communist?"

"I believe that, yes. I shan't see the day, of course."

"The victory of the proletariat will be complete?"

"Yes."

"All the world will be like Russia?"

"I didn't say that. Russia is not yet Communist. It has only advanced along the road to Communism farther than other countries." He put a friendly hand against Father Quixote's mouth. "Don't you, a Catholic, start talking to me about human rights and I promise that I won't talk to you about the Inquisition. If Spain had been entirely Catholic, of course, there would have been no Inquisition—but the Church had to defend herself against enemies. In a war there is always injustice. Men will always have to choose a lesser evil and the lesser evil may mean the state, the prison camp, yes, if you like to say it, the psychiatric hospital. The state or the Church is on the defensive, but when we arrive at Communism, the state will wither away. Just as, if your Church had been successful in making a Catholic world, the Holy Office would have withered away."

"Suppose Communism arrives and you are still alive."

"That's an impossibility."

"Well, imagine you had a great-great-grandson of the same character as yours and he lived to see the end of the state. No injustice, no inequality—how would he spend his life, Sancho?"

"Working for the common good."

"You certainly have faith, Sancho, great faith in the future. But *he* would have no faith. The future would be there before his eyes. Can a man live without faith?"

"I don't know what you mean—without faith. There will always be things for a man to do. The discovery of new energy. And disease—there will always be disease to fight."

"Are you sure? Medicine is making great strides. I feel sorry for your great-great-grandson, Sancho. It seems to me that he may have nothing to hope for except death."

The Mayor smiled. "Perhaps we shall even conquer death with transplants."

"God forbid," Father Quixote said. "Then he would be living in a desert without end. No doubt. No faith. I would prefer him to have what we call a happy death."

"What do you mean by a happy death?"

"I mean the hope of something further."

"The beatific vision and all that nonsense? Believing in some life eternal?"

"No. Not necessarily believing. We can't always believe. Just having faith. Like you have, Sancho. Oh, Sancho,

Sancho, it's an awful thing not to have doubts. Suppose all Marx wrote was *proved* to be absolute truth, and Lenin's works too."

"I'd be glad, of course."

"I wonder."

They drove for a while in silence. Suddenly Sancho gave the same yapping laugh that Father Quixote had heard in the night.

"What is it, Sancho?"

"Last night before I slept I was reading your Jone and his *Moral Theology*. I had forgotten that onanism contained such a rich variety of sins. I had thought of it as just another word for masturbation."

"A very common mistake. But you should have known better, Sancho. You told me you studied at Salamanca."

"Yes. And I remembered last night how we all used to laugh when we came to onanism."

"I had forgotten Jone was so funny."

"Let me remind you of his remarks on *coitus interruptus*. That is one of the forms of onanism according to Jone, but in his view it is not a sin if done on account of some unforeseen necessity, for example (it's Jone's own example) the arrival of a third person on the scene. Well, one of my fellow students, Diego, knew a very rich and pious stockbroker. His name comes back to me—Marquez. He had a big estate across the river from Salamanca, not far from where the Vincentians have their monastery. I wonder if he is still alive. Well, if he is, birth control will no longer be a problem—he must be over eighty. But certainly it was a terrible problem to him in those days, for he was a great stickler for the rules of the Church. It was lucky for him that the Church had altered the rules about usury, for there's a lot of usury in stockbroking. It's funny, isn't it, but the Church can alter its mind about what concerns money much more easily than it can about what concerns sex."

"You have your unalterable dogmas too."

"Yes. But with us the dogmas which are the most impossible to alter are just those that deal with money. We don't worry about *coitus interruptus*, only about the means of production—I don't mean sexually. Please, at the next turning, take the road to the left. Now do you see ahead the high rocky hill with a great cross on top? That's where we are going."

"Then it *is* a holy site. I thought you were making fun of me."

"No, no, monsignor. I am too fond of you for that. What was I talking about? Oh, I remember. Señor Marquez and his terrible problem. He had five children. He really felt he had done his duty to the Church, but his wife was terribly fecund and he enjoyed sex. He could have taken a mistress, but I don't think Jone would allow birth control even in adultery. What you call natural birth control and what I call unnatural had consistently failed him. Perhaps the thermometers in Spain have been falsified under clerical influence. Well, my friend Diego mentioned to him—I'm afraid in a frivolous moment—that *coitus interruptus* was permissible according to the rules of Jone. By the way, what sort of a priest was Jone?"

"He was German. I don't think he was a secular; they are most of them too busy to be moral theologians."

"Marquez listened to Diego, and the next time Diego went to his house he found that a butler had been installed. This surprised him, for Marquez was a mean man who did little entertaining apart from an occasional father from the Vincentian monastery, and two maidservants, a nurse, and a cook were quite enough for the household. After dinner Marquez invited Diego to his study for a glass of brandy, and this surprised Diego too. 'I have to thank you,' Marquez told him, 'for you have made my life much easier for me. I have been reading Father Jone with great care. I 75 admit that I didn't quite trust what you told me, but I have obtained a copy in Spanish from the Vincentians, and there it certainly is, with the imprimatur of the Archbishop of Madrid and a *Nihil Obstat* from the Censor Deputatus— the arrival of a third person does make a *coitus interruptus* permissible.'

" 'How does that help you?' Diego asked.

" 'You see I have hired a butler, and I have trained him very carefully. When a bell in my bedroom rings twice in the pantry he takes up position outside the bedroom door and waits. I try not to keep him waiting too long, but with advancing age I'm afraid that I sometimes keep him there for a quarter of an hour or more before the next signal—a prolonged peal of the bell in the passage itself. That is when I feel unable to contain myself much longer. The butler opens the door immediately and at this arrival of a third person I withdraw at once from the body of my wife. You can't think how Jone has simplified life for me. Now I don't have to go to confession more than once in three months for very venial little matters.' "

"You are mocking me," Father Quixote said.

"Not a bit of it. I find Jone a much more interesting and amusing writer than I did when I was a student. Unfortunately in this particular case there was a snag and Diego was unkind enough to point it out. 'You read Jone carelessly,' Diego told Marquez. 'Jone qualifies the arrival of a third person by classing it as "an unforeseen necessity." I'm afraid in your case the butler's arrival has been only too well foreseen.' Poor Marquez was shattered. Oh, you can't beat those moral theologians. They get the better of you every time with their quibbles. It's better not to listen to them at all. I would like for your sake to clear your shelves of all those old books. Remember what the canon said to your noble ancestor. 'Nor is it reasonable for a man like yourself, possessed of your understanding, your reputation and your talents, to accept all the extravagant absurdities in these ridiculous books of chivalry as really true.' "

The Mayor stopped speaking and glanced sideways at Father Quixote. He said, "Your face has certainly something in common with that of your ancestor. If I am Sancho you are surely the Monsignor of the Sorrowful Countenance."

"You can mock *me* as much as you like, Sancho. What makes me sad is when you mock my books, for they mean much more to me than myself. They are all the faith I have and all the hope."

"In return for Father Jone I will lend you Father Lenin. Perhaps he will give you hope too."

"Hope in this world perhaps, but I have a greater hunger —and not for myself alone. For you, Sancho, and all our world. I know I'm a poor priest errant, traveling God knows where. I know that there are absurdities in some of my books as there were in the books of chivalry my ancestor collected. That didn't mean that all chivalry was absurd. Whatever absurdities you can dig out of my books, I still have faith. . . ."

"In what?"

"In a historic fact. That Christ died on the Cross and rose again."

"The greatest absurdity of all."

"It's an absurd world or we wouldn't be here together."

They had reached the height of the Guadarramas, a hard climb for Rocinante, and now they descended towards a valley under a high somber hill which was surmounted by the huge heavy cross which must have been nearly a hundred and fifty meters high; they could see ahead of them a park full of cars—rich Cadillacs and little Seats. The Seat owners had put up folding tables by their cars for a picnic.

"Would you want to live in a wholly rational world?" Father Quixote asked. "What a dull world that would be."

"There speaks your ancestor."

"Look at the guillotine on top of the hill—or the gallows if you prefer."

"I see a cross."

"That's more or less the same thing, isn't it? Where are we, Sancho?"

"This is the Valley of the Fallen, father. Here your friend Franco like a pharaoh planned to be buried. More than a thousand prisoners were forced to excavate his tomb."

"Oh yes, I remember, and they were given their liberty in return."

"For hundreds it was the liberty of death. Shall you say a prayer here, father?"

"Of course. Why not? Even if it were the tomb of Judas —or Stalin—I'd say a prayer."

They parked the car at a cost of sixty pesetas and came to the entrance. What a rock it would need, Father Quixote thought, to close this enormous tomb. At the entrance a metal grille was decorated with the statues of forty Spanish saints, and inside stretched a hall the size of a cathedral nave, the walls covered with what appeared to be sixteenth-century tapestries. "The Generalissimo insisted on the whole brigade of saints," the Mayor said. The visitors and their voices were diminished by the size of the hall, and it seemed a long walk to the altar at the end under a great dome.

"A remarkable engineering feat," the Mayor said, "like the pyramids. And it needed slave labor to accomplish it."

"As in your Siberian camps."

"Russian prisoners labor at least for the future of their country. This was for the glory of one man."

They walked at a slow pace towards the altar, passing chapel after chapel. No one in this richly decorated hall felt the need to lower his voice, and yet the voices sounded as soft as whispers in the immensity. It was difficult to believe that they were walking inside a mountain.

"As I understood it," Father Quixote said, "this was meant to be a chapel of reconciliation where all the fallen on both sides were to be remembered."

On one side of the altar was the grave of Franco, on the other the grave of José Antonio Primo de Rivera, the founder of the Falange.

"You won't find even a tablet for the dead Republicans," the Mayor said.

They were silent as they took the long way back to the entrance, and from there they gave a last glance behind. "A little like the hall of the Palace Hotel," the Mayor said, "but of course much grander and fewer guests. The Palace Hotel could not afford those tapestries. And down there at the end you can see the cocktail bar waiting for the barman to shake a drink—the specialty of the bar is a cocktail of red wine taken with wafer biscuits. You are silent, monsignor. Surely you find it impressive. Is something wrong?"

"I was praying, that's all," Father Quixote said.

"For the Generalissimo buried in his grandeur?"

"Yes. Also for you and me." He added, "And for my Church." As they drove away Father Quixote made the sign of the cross. He was not himself sure why, whether it was as a protection against the perils of the road or against hasty judgments, or just a nervous reaction.

The Mayor said, "I have an impression we are being followed." He leaned across Father Quixote to look into the mirror. "Everybody is overtaking your car except for one."

"Why should we be followed?"

"Who knows? I asked you to put on your purple bib."

"I did put on the socks."

"They are not enough."

"Where are we going now?"

"At your speed we will never get to Salamanca tonight. We had better stay at Avila." The Mayor, watching in the mirror, added, "At last he's overtaken us." A car went by at high speed.

"You see, Sancho, they weren't concerned with us."

"It was a jeep. A jeep of the Guardia."

"Anyway, they hadn't us in mind."

"All the same, I wish you had been wearing your bib," the Mayor said. "They can't see your socks."

They had lunch by the road and sitting on the withered grass finished up what was left of the sausage. It was getting a bit dry and somehow the Manchegan wine had lost much of its flavor.

"I am reminded by the sausage," the Mayor said, "that at Avila you will be able to see if you want the ring finger of Saint Teresa, and at Alba de Tormes, near Salamanca, I can show you a whole hand of hers. At least I believe it has been returned by now to the convent there—it was borrowed for a time by the Generalissimo. They say he kept it —with all reverence of course—on his desk. And at Avila there is the confessional where she used to talk to Saint John of the Cross. A great poet so we won't argue about his sanctity. When I was staying in Salamanca I used often to visit Avila. Do you know that I even felt a sort of reverence for that ring finger, though my chief attraction was a most beautiful girl—she was the daughter of a chemist in Avila."

"What made you drop your studies, Sancho? You've never told me that."

"I think that perhaps her long golden hair was the main reason. It was a very happy period. You see, as the daughter of the chemist—he was a secret member of the Party— she was able to supply us with his clandestine contraceptives. I didn't have to practice *coitus interruptus*. But do you know—human nature is a strange thing—I would go afterwards and say I was sorry to the ring finger of Saint

Teresa." He stared gloomily into his glass of wine. "Oh, I laugh at your superstitions, father, but I shared some of them in those days. Is that why I seek your company now —to find my youth again, that youth when I half believed in your religion and everything was so complicated and contradictory—and interesting?"

"I never found things so complicated. I have always discovered the answer in the books you despise."

"Even in Father Jone?"

"Oh, I was never very strong at moral theology."

"One of my problems was that the girl's father, the chemist, died, and so we could no longer get the contraceptives. Today it would be easy enough, but in those days. . . . Have another glass of wine, father."

"In your company I fear if I'm not careful I shall become what I've heard called a whiskey priest."

"I can say, like my ancestor Sancho, that I've never drunk out of vice in my life. I drink when I have a fancy and to toast a friend. Here's to you, monsignor. What does Father Jone say about drinking?"

"Intoxication that ends in complete loss of reason is a mortal sin unless there is a sufficient reason, and making others drink is the same unless there is a sufficient excuse."

"How he qualifies things, doesn't he?"

"Curiously enough, according to Father Jone, it is more readily permissible to be the occasion of another's drunkenness—what you are guilty of now—at a banquet."

"I suppose we could regard this as a banquet?"

"I am not at all sure whether two can make a banquet and I wonder whether our rather dry sausage qualifies." Father Quixote laughed a little nervously (humor was perhaps not quite in place) and he felt the rosary in his pocket. He said, "You may laugh at Father Jone, and I have laughed with you, God forgive me. But, Sancho, moral theology is not the Church. And Father Jone is not among my old books of chivalry. His book is only like a book of military regulations. Saint Francis de Sales wrote a book of eight hundred pages on the love of God. The word love doesn't come into Father Jone's rules and I think, perhaps I am wrong, that you won't find the phrase 'mortal sin' in Saint Francis's book. He was the Bishop and Prince of Geneva. I wonder how he and Calvin would have got along. I think Calvin would have been more at home with Lenin—even Stalin. Or the Guardia Civil," he added watching the jeep returning—if it was the same jeep. His ancestor would have gone out into the road and challenged it perhaps. He felt his own inadequacy and even a sense of guilt. The jeep slowed down as it passed their car. They both had a sense of relief when it went on out of their sight and they lay for a while in silence among the debris of their meal. Then Father Quixote said, "We have done nothing wrong, Sancho."

"They judge by appearances."

"But we look as innocent as lambs," Father Quixote said and he quoted his favorite saint, " 'Nothing appeases an enraged elephant so much as a sight of a little lamb, and nothing breaks the force of cannonballs so well as wool.' "

"Whoever wrote that," the Mayor said, "showed his ignorance of natural history and dynamics."

"I suppose it's the wine, but I feel extremely hot."

"I can't say that I notice the heat. It seems to me a very agreeable temperature. But of course I am not wearing one of those absurd collars."

"A bit of celluloid. It's not really at all hot, when you think what those Guardia are wearing. Just try and you'll see."

"All right, I will. Give it me. If I remember right, Sancho became governor of an island, and so with your help I will become a governor of souls. Like Father Jone." He balanced the collar round his neck. "No. You are right. It doesn't seem so hot. A bit constricting, that's all. It rubs a sore place on my neck. How odd, father, without your collar I would never take you for a priest and certainly not for a monsignor."

"When his housekeeper took away his spear and stripped Don Quixote of his armor you would never have taken him for a knight errant. Only for a crazy old man. Give me back my collar, Sancho."

"Let me be a governor for just a little while longer. Perhaps with this collar I might even hear a confession or two."

Father Quixote put out his hand to snatch the collar when a voice of authority spoke. "Show me your papers." It was the Guardia. He must have left his jeep round a bend in the road and then approached them on foot. He was a stout man and he was sweating from exhaustion or apprehension, for his fingers played on his holster. Perhaps he was afraid of a Basque terrorist.

Father Quixote said, "My wallet is in the car."

"We will fetch it together. And yours, father," he demanded of Sancho.

Sancho felt in his breast pocket for his identity card.

"What is that heavy object in your pocket?"

The Guardia's hand rested on his gun as Sancho removed a small green volume marked *Moral Theology*. "Not forbidden reading, officer."

"I have not said it was, father."

"I am not a father, officer."

"Then why are you wearing that collar?"

"I borrowed it for a moment from my friend. Look. It's not attached. Just balanced. My friend is a monsignor."

"A monsignor?"

"Yes, you can see that by his socks." The Guardia took a look at the purple socks. He asked, "This book is yours then? And the collar?"

"Yes," Father Quixote said.

"You lent them to this man?"

"Yes. You see, I was feeling hot and. . . ." The Guardia signaled him to the car.

Father Quixote opened the glove compartment. For a moment he couldn't see his identity card. The Guardia breathed heavily behind him. Then Father Quixote noticed that, perhaps impelled by the heavy panting of a tired Rocinante, the card had slipped between the red covers of a book which the Mayor had left there. He pulled the book out. The author's name was marked in heavy type: LENIN.

"Lenin," the Guardia exclaimed. "Is this book yours?"

"No, no. Mine is the moral theology one."

"Is this your car?"

"Yes."

"But this is not your book?"

"It belongs to my friend here."

"The man to whom you lent your collar?"

"That's right."

The Mayor had followed them to the car. His voice made the Guardia jump. It was obvious that the man's nerves were not in a good state. "Even Lenin is not forbidden reading now, Guardia. This is quite an early work—his essays on Marx and Engels. Written mainly in the respectable city of Zurich. You might say—a little time-bomb made in the city of bankers."

"A time-bomb," the Guardia exclaimed.

"I am talking metaphorically."

The Guardia laid down the book with caution on the seat and moved a little away from the car. He said to Father Quixote, "There is nothing on your identity card about your being a monsignor."

"He is traveling incognito," the Mayor said.

"Incognito. Why incognito?"

"He has the kind of humility which is often to be found in holy men."

"Where have you come from?"

"He has been praying at the tomb of the Generalissimo."

"Is that true?"

"Well, yes, I did say a few prayers."

The Guardia examined the card again. He looked a little reassured.

"Several prayers," the Mayor said. "One would hardly be enough."

"What do you mean—not enough?"

"God can be hard of hearing. I am not a believer myself, but, as I understand it, that must have been the reason why there were so many Masses said for the Generalissimo. For a man like that one you have to shout to be heard."

"You keep strange company," the Guardia told Father Quixote.

"Oh, you mustn't pay attention to what he says. He is a good man at heart."

"Where are you going now?"

The Mayor spoke first. "The monsignor wants to say another prayer for the Generalissimo to the ring finger of Saint Teresa. You know the finger is kept in the convent outside the walls of Avila. He wants to do his best for the Generalissimo."

"You talk too much. Your card says you are the Mayor of El Toboso."

"I *was* the Mayor, but I have lost my job. And the monsignor has been promoted out of his."

"Where did you spend last night?"

"In Madrid."

"Where? What hotel?"

Father Quixote looked at the Mayor for help. He said, "A little place—I don't remember—"

"What street?"

The Mayor interrupted firmly, "The Palace Hotel."

"That's not a little place."

"Size is relative," the Mayor said. "The Palace Hotel is a very small place if you compare it to the Generalissimo's tomb."

There was an uneasy silence—perhaps an angel was passing overhead. At last, "Stay here," the Guardia said, "until I come back. If you try to start the car you will get hurt."

"What does he mean—I will get hurt?"

"I think he is threatening to shoot us if we move."

"So we stay."

"We stay."

"Why did you lie about the hotel?"

"Hesitation would only make things worse."

"But they can check the *ficha*."

"They may not bother and anyway it will take time."

"To me," Father Quixote said, "this is an inexplicable situation. Not in all my years in El Toboso. . . ."

"It wasn't until he left his village that your ancestor encountered the windmills. Look. Our task is easier. We have not thirty or forty windmills to encounter, we have only two."

The fat Guardia, who was returning with his companion, certainly brought a windmill to mind by the way he waved his arms as he explained to his companion the strange contradictions he had encountered. The words "monsignor," "Lenin," and "purple socks" came to them over the slight afternoon breeze.

The second Guardia was very thin and decisive in his manner. "Open the boot," he commanded. He stood with his hands on his hips while Father Quixote fumbled with his key.

"Open your bag."

He put his hand in Father Quixote's bag and pulled out a purple *pechera*. "Why are you not wearing this?" he asked.

"It's too noticeable," Father Quixote replied.

"You are afraid to be noticed?"

"Not afraid. . . ." But the thin Guardia was already looking through the rear window.

"What are those boxes?"

"Manchegan wine."

"You seem very well supplied."

"Yes indeed. If you would care for a couple of bottles. . . ."

"Write down," the Guardia told his companion, "the so-called monsignor offered us two bottles of Manchegan wine. Let me see his identity card. Have you noted the number?"

"I will do so at once."

"Let me look at that book." He ruffled through the pages of Lenin's essays. "I see you have studied this well," he said. "Many passages have been marked. Published in Moscow in Spanish." He began to read: " 'Armed struggle pursues two different aims: in the first place the struggle aims at assassinating individuals, chiefs and subordinates in the army and police. . . .' Are these your aims, monsignor—if you are a monsignor?"

"That book doesn't belong to me. It belongs to my friend."

"You keep strange company, monsignor. Dangerous company." He stood in silent thought—to Father Quixote he looked like a judge who is pondering the alternative of a death sentence or perpetual imprisonment. Father Quixote said, "If you care to telephone to my bishop. . . ." But he stopped in mid-sentence, for the bishop would certainly remember the imprudent church collection for the society In Vinculis.

"You have the number of the car?" the thin Guardia said to the fat Guardia.

"Oh yes, yes, of course. I took it while we were on the road."

"You go to Avila? Where will you be staying in Avila?"

The Mayor said quickly, "At the *parador*. If they have rooms."

"You have no reservations?"

"We are on holiday, Guardia. We take the luck of the road."

"And I have taken the number of your car," the Guardia said. The thin one turned and the fat one followed him. In their walk Father Quixote thought they resembled two ducks—one ready for the table and one needing more nourishment. They went round the bend of road out of sight—perhaps the pond was there.

"We will wait till they drive away," the Mayor said.

"What is wrong with us, Sancho? Why are they so suspicious?"

"You must admit," the Mayor said, "that it is not very usual for a monsignor to lend his clerical collar. . . ."

"I will follow after them and explain."

"No, no, better to wait here. They are waiting too. To see whether we are really going to Avila."

"Then to show them that we are, let us drive on—to Avila."

"I think it would be better to avoid Avila."

"Why?"

"They will have already warned the Guardia there."

"Of what? We are innocent. We are doing harm to no one."

"We are doing harm to their peace of mind. Let them get tired of waiting. I think we should open another bottle of wine."

They settled again among the debris of their meal and the Mayor began to pull a cork. He said, "If I could suspend my profound disbelief in God, I would still find it hard to believe that he really wanted those two Guardia to be born —not to speak of Hitler and the Generalissimo or, if you like, of Stalin. If only their poor parents had been permitted to use a contraceptive. . . ."

"That would have been a grave sin, Sancho. To kill a human soul. . . ."

"Has sperm a soul? When a man makes love he kills a million million spermatozoa—minus one. It's lucky for Heaven that there's such a lot of waste or it might become severely overpopulated."

"But it is against the Law of Nature, Sancho."

The cork came out with a pop—it was a very young wine.

"I have always been mystified about the Law of Nature," Sancho said. "What law? What nature?"

"It is the law which was put into our hearts at birth. Our conscience tells us when we break the law."

"Mine doesn't. Or I've never noticed it. Who invented the law?"

"God."

"Oh yes, of course you would say that, but let me put it in another way. What human first taught us that it existed?"

"From the very earliest days of Christianity—"

"Come, come, monsignor. Can you find anything about natural law in Saint Paul?"

"Alas, Sancho, I don't remember, I grow old, but I am sure. . . ."

"The law of nature as I see it, father, is that a cat has a natural desire to kill a bird or a mouse. All right for the cat, but not so good for the bird or the mouse."

"Mockery is not an argument, Sancho."

"Oh, I don't deny the conscience altogether, monsignor. I would feel uneasy, I suppose, for a time if I killed a man without adequate reason, but I think I would feel uneasy for a whole lifetime if I fathered an unwanted child."

"We must trust in the mercy of God."

"He's not always so merciful, is he, not in Africa or India?

And even in our own country if the child has to live in poverty, disease, probably without any chance—"

"The chance of eternal happiness," Father Quixote said.

"Oh yes, and according to your Church the chance also of eternal misery. If his circumstances give him a turn to what you call evil."

The reference to Hell closed Father Quixote's lips. "I believe, I believe," he told himself, "I must believe," but he thought too of the silence of Saint John, like the silence in the eye of a tornado. And was it the Devil who reminded him of how the Romans, according to Saint Augustine, had a god called Vaticanus, "the god of children's crying"? He said, "You have helped yourself to a glass of wine but not me."

"Hold out your glass then. Is there a little cheese left?" Father Quixote searched among the rubble. "A man can restrain his appetite," he said.

"The cheese?"

"No, no. I meant his sexual appetite."

"Is that control natural? Perhaps for you and the Pope in Rome, but for two people who love each other and live together and have hardly enough to eat themselves, leave alone a young brat with an appetite. . . ."

It was the age-old argument and he had no convincing answer. "There are natural means," he said as he had said a hundred times before, aware only of the extent of his ignorance.

"Who but moral theologians would call them natural? So many days in each month in which to make love, but first you must put in your thermometer and take the temperature. . . . It's not the way desire works."

Father Quixote remembered a phrase from one of the old books he valued most, Augustine's *City of God*: "The motion will sometimes be importunate against the will, and sometimes immovable when it is desired, and being fervent in the mind, yet will be frozen in the body. Thus wondrously does this lust fail man." It was not a hope to be relied on.

"I suppose that your Father Heribert Jone would say that to make love with your wife in safety after her menopause was a form of masturbation."

"Perhaps he would, poor man."

Poor man? He thought: At least Saint Augustine wrote of sex from experience and not from theory: he was a sinner and a saint, he was not a moral theologian. He was a poet and even a humorist. As students how they had laughed at one passage in *The City of God*: "There are those that can break wind backward so artificially that you would think they sung." What would Father Heribert Jone have thought of that? It was difficult to visualize a moral theologian having his morning stool.

"Give me another bit of cheese," Father Quixote said. "Listen. Here comes the jeep."

The jeep drove slowly past them. The fat Guardia was at the wheel and the thin one looked penetratingly towards them as though he were a naturalist observing two rare insects which he must remember to describe with accuracy. Father Quixote felt glad that he was again wearing his clerical collar. He even pushed out a foot to show the purple socks which he hated.

"We have conquered the windmills," the Mayor said.

"What windmills?"

"The Guardia revolve with every wind. They were there with the Generalissimo. They are there now. If my party came to power they would still be there, turning with the wind from the east."

"Shall we take the road again now they are gone?"

"Not yet. I want to see if they come back."

"If you don't want them to follow us to Avila, what way shall we take?"

"I'm sorry to deprive you of Saint Teresa's ring finger, but I think Segovia would be better. Tomorrow we will visit in Salamanca a holier shrine than the one you prayed at today."

The first chill of the evening had touched them. The Mayor moved restlessly to the road and back again: no sign of the Guardia. He said, "Were you never in love with a woman, father?"

"Never. Not in the way you mean."

"Were you never tempted . . . ?"

"Never."

"Strange and inhuman."

"It's not so strange or inhuman," Father Quixote replied. "I have been protected like many others. It is a little like the taboo of incest. Not many are tempted to break that."

"No, but there are always so many alternatives to incest. Like a friend's sister."

"I had my alternative too."

"Who was she?"

"A girl called Martin."

"She was your Dulcinea?"

"Yes, if you like, but she lived a very long way from El Toboso. All the same her letters reached me there. They were a great comfort to me when things were difficult with the bishop. There was one thing she wrote—I think of it nearly every day: 'Before we die by the sword, let us die by pin stabs.' "

"Your ancestor would have preferred the sword."

"All the same, perhaps, in the end it was by pin stabs that he died."

"Martin—from the way you pronounce it she was not a Spanish girl?"

"No, she was a Norman. You mustn't misunderstand me. She was dead many years before I knew her and grew to love her. You have heard of her perhaps under another name. She lived at Lisieux. The Carmelites there had a special vocation—to pray for priests. I hope—I think—she prays for me."

"Oh, you are talking about that Sainte Thérèse—the name Martin confused me."

"I'm glad there's a Communist who has heard of her."

"You know, I was not always a Communist."

"Well, anyway, perhaps a true Communist is a sort of priest, and in that case she prays undoubtedly for you."

"It's cold waiting around here. Let's be off."

They drove for a while in silence back along the road they had come. There was no sign of the jeep. They passed the turning to Avila and followed the sign toward Segovia. The Mayor said at last, "So that is your love story, father. Mine is rather different, except that the woman is dead too, like yours."

"God rest her soul," Father Quixote said. It was an automatic reflex when he spoke, but in the silence that descended on both of them he prayed to the unknown woman as he was accustomed to pray to the souls in Purgatory: 'You are nearer God than I am. Pray for us both.' "

The great Roman aqueduct of Segovia loomed ahead of them, casting a long shadow in the evening light.

They found a lodging in a small *albergue* not far from the Church of Saint Martin—that name again, the name by which he always thought of her. She seemed closer to him then than in her trappings as a saint or under her sentimental nickname of the Little Flower. He would even sometimes address her in his prayers as Señorita Martin as though the family name might catch her ear through all the thousands of incantations addressed to her in all tongues by the light of candles before the plaster image.

They had drunk enough by the roadside and neither was in the mood to seek a restaurant. It was as though two dead women had been traveling with them during those last kilometers. Father Quixote was glad to have a room to himself, minute though it was. It seemed to him that his journey had already extended across the whole breadth of Spain, though he knew he was not much more than two hundred kilometers from La Mancha. The slowness of Rocinante made a nonsense of distance. Well, the farthest that his ancestor had gone from La Mancha in all his journeys had been the city of Barcelona and yet anyone who had read the true history would have thought that Don Quixote had covered the whole immense area of Spain. There is a virtue in slowness which we have lost. Rocinante was of more value for a true traveler than a jet plane. Jet planes were for businessmen.

Before he went to sleep Father Quixote read a little because he was still haunted by his dream. He opened as was his custom Saint Francis de Sales at random. Even before the birth of Christ men had taken the *sortes Virgilianae* as a kind of horoscope and he had more faith in Saint Francis than in Virgil, that rather derivative poet. What he found in *The Love of God* astonished him a little, but all the same it encouraged him. "Among the reflections and resolutions it is good to make use of colloquies, and speak sometimes to our Lord, sometimes to the Angels, to the Saints and to oneself, to one's own heart, to sinners, and even to inanimate creatures. . . ." He said to Rocinante, "Forgive me. I have driven you too hard," and fell into a dreamless sleep.

VI

HOW MONSIGNOR QUIXOTE AND SANCHO VISIT ANOTHER HOLY SITE

I am glad," the Mayor said as they took the road to Sala-manca, "that you have at last consented to put on that bib —what do you call it?"

"A *pechera*."

"I was afraid that we might find ourselves in prison if those Guardia checked too quickly in Avila."

"Why? For what?"

"The reason is unimportant, it's only the fact which counts. I had some experience of prison during the Civil War. There was always a certain tension in prison, you know. One's friends went away and never came back."

"But now—there's no war now. Things are better."

"Yes. Perhaps. Of course, in Spain one finds that all the best people have been for a while in prison. It's possible that we would never have heard of your great ancestor if Cervantes had not served his time that way more than once. The prison gives you even more chance to think than a monastery where the poor devils have to wake up at all sorts of ungodly hours to pray. In prison I was never woken up before six o'clock and at night the lights went out usually at nine. Of course interrogations were apt to be painful, but they took place at a reasonable hour. Never during the siesta. The great thing to remember, monsignor, is that unlike an abbot an interrogator wants to sleep at his usual hour."

In Arévalo there were some old torn posters of a traveling circus on the walls. A man in tights displayed arms and thighs of an exorbitant size. El Tigre he was called, "The Great Wrestler of the Pyrenees."

"How little Spain changes," the Mayor said. "You would never feel in France that you were in the world of Racine or Molière, nor in London that you were still close to Shakespeare's time. It is only in Spain and Russia that time stands still. We shall have our adventures on the road, father, much as your ancestor did. We have already battled with the windmills and we have only missed by a week or two an adventure with the Tiger. He would probably have proved as tame when challenged as your ancestor found the lion."

"But I am not Don Quixote, Sancho. I would be afraid to challenge a man of such a size."

"You underrate yourself, father. Your faith is your spear. If the Tiger had dared to say something derogatory of your beloved Dulcinea. . . ."

"But you know I have no Dulcinea, Sancho."

"I was referring of course to Señorita Martin."

Another poster which they passed exhibited a tattooed lady almost as large as the Tiger. "Spain has always loved monsters," Sancho said and he gave his strange yapping laugh. "What would you do, father, if you had to be present at the birth of a monster with two heads?"

"I would baptize it of course. What an absurd question."

"But you would be wrong, monsignor. Remember I have been reading Father Heribert Jone. He teaches that if you doubt whether you are dealing with one monster or two, you must strike an average and baptize one head absolutely and the other conditionally."

"Really, Sancho, I am not responsible for Father Jone. You seem to have read him far more closely than I have ever done."

"And in the case of a difficult birth, father, when some other part than the head is presented first, you must baptize that, so I suppose that in the case of a breech birth. . . ."

"Tonight, Sancho, I promise you that I will take up the study of Marx and Lenin if you will leave Father Jone alone."

"Then begin with Marx and *The Communist Manifesto*. The *Manifesto* is short and Marx is a much better writer than Lenin."

They crossed the river Tormes into the gray old city of Salamanca in the early afternoon. Father Quixote was still unaware of the object of their pilgrimage, but he was happy in his ignorance. This was the university city where he had as a boy dreamt of making his studies. Here he could visit the actual lecture room where the great Saint John of the Cross attended the classes of the theologian Fray Luis de León, and Fray Luis might well have known his own ancestor if the Don's travels had taken him to Salamanca. Looking up at the great carved gateway of the university, with the chiseled Pope surrounded by his cardinals, the heads in medallion of all the Catholic kings, where even Venus and Hercules had been found a place, not to mention a very small frog, he muttered a prayer. The frog had been pointed out by two children who demanded payment in return.

"What did you say, father?"

"This is a holy city, Sancho."

"You feel at home here, don't you? Here in the library are all your books of chivalry in their first editions, moldering away in old calf. I doubt if any student draws one out to blow the dust away."

"How lucky you were to study here, Sancho."

"Lucky? I'm not so sure of that. I feel very much an exile now. Perhaps we should have traveled east towards the home I've never known. To the future, not to the past. Not to the home I left."

"You went through this very doorway to your lectures. I'm trying to imagine the young Sancho. . . ."

"They were not lectures by Father Heribert Jone."

"Wasn't there at least one professor whom you were prepared to listen to?"

"Oh yes. In those days I still had a half belief. A complete believer I could never have listened to for long, but there was one professor with a half belief and I listened to him for two years. Perhaps I would have lasted longer at Salamanca if he had stayed, but he went into exile—as he had already done years before. He wasn't a Communist, I doubt if he was a Socialist, but he couldn't swallow the Generalissimo. So here we've come to see what's left of him."

In a very small square, above faceless folds of rumpled green-black stone, an aggressive head with a pointed beard stared upwards at the shutters of a little house. "That's where he died," Sancho said, "in a room up there sitting with a friend before a charcoal-burner to keep him warm. His friend saw suddenly that one of his slippers was on fire and yet Unamuno had not stirred. You can still see the stigmata of the burnt shoe in the wooden floor."

"Unamuno." Father Quixote repeated the name and looked up with respect at the face of stone, the hooded eyes expressing the fierceness and the arrogance of individual thought.

"You know how he loved your ancestor and studied his life. If he had lived in those days perhaps he would have followed the Don on the mule called Dapple, instead of Sancho. Many priests gave a sigh of relief when they heard of his death. Perhaps even the Pope in Rome felt easier without him. And Franco too, of course, if he was intelligent enough to recognize the strength of his enemy. In a sense he was my enemy too for he kept me in the Church for several years with that half belief of his which for a while I could share."

"And now you have a complete belief, don't you? In the prophet Marx. You don't have to think for yourself any more. Isaiah has spoken. You are in the hands of future history. How happy you must be with your complete belief. There's only one thing you will ever lack—the dignity of despair." Father Quixote spoke with an unaccustomed anger—or was it, he wondered, envy?

"Have I complete belief?" Sancho asked. "Sometimes I wonder. The ghost of my professor haunts me. I dream I am sitting in his lecture room and he is reading to us from one of his own books. I hear him saying, 'There is a muffled voice, a voice of uncertainty which whispers in the ears of the believer. Who knows? Without this uncertainty how could we live?' "

"He wrote that?"

"Yes."

They returned to Rocinante.

"Where do we go from here, Sancho?"

"We go to the cemetery. You will find his tomb rather different from the Generalissimo's."

It was a rough road out to the cemetery on the extreme edge of the city—not a smooth road for a hearse to travel. The body, Father Quixote thought, as Rocinante groaned when the gears changed, would have had a good shaking up before it reached the quiet ground; but as he soon discovered there had been no quiet ground left for a new body —the earth was fully occupied by the proud tombs of generations before. At the gates they were given a number, as in the cloakroom of a museum or a restaurant, and they walked down the long white wall in which boxes had been inserted half a dozen deep till they reached number 340.

"I prefer this to the Generalissimo's mountain," Sancho said. "When I am alone, I sleep more easily in a small bed."

As they walked back to the car Sancho asked, "Did you say a prayer?"

"Of course."

"The same prayer as you said for the Generalissimo?"

"There's only one prayer we need say for anyone dead."

"So you'd say it for Stalin?"

"Of course."

"And for Hitler?"

"There are degrees of evil, Sancho—and of good. We can try to discriminate between the living, but with the dead we can't discriminate. They all have the same need of our prayer."

VII

HOW IN SALAMANCA MONSIGNOR QUIXOTE CONTINUED HIS STUDIES

The hotel in which they lodged in Salamanca was in a little gray side street. It seemed quiet and friendly to Father Quixote. His knowledge of hotels was necessarily limited, but there were several things about this hotel which particularly pleased him and he expressed his pleasure to Sancho when they were alone and he was sitting on Sancho's bed on the first floor. Father Quixote had been lodged on the third, "where it will be quieter" the manageress had told him.

"The *patrona* was truly welcoming," Father Quixote said, "unlike that poor old woman in Madrid, and what a large staff of charming young women for so small a hotel."

"In a university city," Sancho said, "there are always a lot of customers."

"And the establishment is so clean. Did you notice how outside every room on the way up to the third floor there was a pile of linen? They must change the linen every evening after the time of siesta. I liked to see too when we arrived the real family atmosphere—all the staff sitting down to an early supper with the *patrona* at the head of the table ladling out the soup. Really she was just like a mother with her daughters."

"She was very impressed at meeting a monsignor."

"And did you notice how she quite forgot to give us a *ficha* to fill in? All she was concerned with was our comfort."

There was a knock on the door. A girl entered with a bottle of champagne in an ice-bucket. She gave Father Quixote a nervous smile and got out of the room again quickly.

"Did you order this, Sancho?"

"No, no. I don't care for champagne. But it's the custom of the house."

"Perhaps we ought to drink a little just to show that we appreciate their kindness."

"Oh, it will be included in the bill. So will their kindness be."

"Don't be a cynic, Sancho. That was a very sweet smile the girl gave us. One can't pay for a smile like that."

"Well, I'll open it if you like. It won't be so good as our Manchegan wine." Sancho began a long struggle between the cork and his thumb, turning his back on Father Quixote for fear of shooting him with the cork. Father Quixote took the opportunity to roam around the room. He said, "What a good idea. They provide a foot-bath."

"What do you mean, a foot-bath? This damn cork won't come out."

"I see a little book of Marx on your bed. May I borrow it to read before I sleep?"

"Of course. It's *The Communist Manifesto* I recommended to you. Much easier to read than *Das Kapital*. I don't think they mean us to drink the champagne. The damned cork won't come out. They'll charge for it just the same."

Father Quixote had always been inquisitive in small ways. His greatest temptation in the confessional box was to ask unnecessary and even irrelevant questions. Now he couldn't resist opening a little square envelope which was lying on Sancho's bedside table—it made him think of his childhood and the tiny letters his mother would sometimes leave for him to read before sleep.

There was an explosion, the cork cracked against the wall, and a fountain of champagne missed the glass. Sancho swore and turned. "What on earth are you doing, father?"

Father Quixote was blowing up a sausage-shaped balloon. He squeezed the end with his fingers. "How do you keep the air in?" he asked. "Surely there should be some sort of nozzle?" He began to blow again and the balloon exploded less loudly though rather more sharply than the champagne bottle. "Oh dear, I'm so sorry, Sancho, I didn't mean to break your balloon. Was it a gift for a child?"

"No, father, it was a gift for the girl who brought the champagne. Don't worry. I've got several more." He added with a kind of anger, "Have you never seen a contraceptive before? No, I suppose you haven't."

"I don't understand. A contraceptive? But what can you do with a thing that size?"

"It wouldn't have been that size if you hadn't blown it up."

Father Quixote sank down on Sancho's bed. He asked, "Where have you brought me, Sancho?"

"To a house that I knew as a student. It's wonderful how these places survive. They are far more stable than dictatorships and war doesn't touch them—even civil war."

"You should never have brought me here. A priest. . . ."

"Don't worry. You won't be bothered in any way. I've explained things to the lady of the house. She understands."

"But why, Sancho, why?"

"I thought it was a good thing to avoid a hotel *ficha* for at least tonight. Those Civil Guards. . . ."

"So we are hiding in a brothel?"

"Yes. You could put it that way."

A most unexpected sound came from the bed. It was the sound of strangled laughter.

Sancho said, "I don't believe I've ever heard you laugh before, father. What's so funny?"

"I'm sorry. It's really very wrong of me to laugh. But I just thought: What would the bishop say if he knew? A monsignor in a brothel. Well, why not? Christ mixed with publicans and sinners. All the same I think I had better go upstairs and lock my door. But be prudent, dear Sancho, be prudent."

"That's what they're for—those things you call balloons. For prudence. I suppose Father Heribert Jone would say that I am adding onanism to fornication."

"Please don't tell me, Sancho, don't ever tell me, about such things. They are private, they belong only to you unless, of course, you wanted to confess."

"What penance would you give me, father, if I came to you in the morning?"

"It's odd, isn't it, but I have had very little practice in dealing with that kind of thing in El Toboso. I am afraid, perhaps, that people are afraid to tell me of anything serious because they meet me every day in the street. You know—of course you don't know—I don't like the taste of tomatoes at all. But suppose Father Heribert Jone had written that it was a mortal sin to eat tomatoes and the old lady who lives next door to me came to me in the church to confess she had eaten a tomato. What penance would I give her? As I don't eat tomatoes myself I wouldn't even be able to imagine how deep her depravity might be. Of course a rule would have been broken . . . a rule . . . one can't avoid knowing that."

"You are avoiding my question, father, what penance . . . ?"

"Perhaps one Our Father and one Hail Mary."

"Only one?"

"One said properly must surely be the equal of a hundred run off without thought. I don't see the point of numbers. We aren't in business as shopkeepers." He lifted himself heavily from the bed.

"Where are you going, father?"

"Off to read myself to sleep with prophet Marx. I wish I could say goodnight to you, Sancho, but I doubt whether yours will be what I would call a good night."

VIII

HOW MONSIGNOR QUIXOTE HAD A CURIOUS ENCOUNTER IN VALLADOLID

Sancho, there was no doubting it, was in a very morose mood. He showed himself unwilling to make any suggestion as to which road they should take out of Salamanca. It was as though he had been soured by the long night that he had spent in the house of his youth. How dangerous it always is to try to recapture in middle age a scene from one's youth, and perhaps he resented also the unusually high spirits shown by Father Quixote. For want of a more cogent reason for going anywhere Father Quixote suggested they take the road to Valladolid in order to see the house where the great biographer Cervantes had completed the life of his forebear. "Unless," he hesitated, "you think we may possibly encounter more windmills on that route?"

"They have more important things to think about than us."

"What?"

"Haven't you read the paper today? A general has been shot in Madrid."

"Who by?"

"In the old days they would have blamed it on the Communists. Thank God, now it's always the Basques and ETA."

"God rest his soul," Father Quixote said.

"You don't need to pity a general."

"I don't pity him. I never pity the dead. I envy them."

Sancho's mood remained. He spoke out only once during the next twenty kilometers and then it was to attack Father Quixote. "Why don't you speak up and say what you think?"

"Think about what?"

"Last night, of course."

"Oh, I'll tell you about last night when we have lunch. I was very pleased with the Marx you lent me. He was a really good man at heart, wasn't he? I was quite surprised by some of the things he wrote. No dull economics."

"I'm not talking about Marx. I'm talking about me."

"You? I hope you slept well?"

"You know perfectly well that I wasn't sleeping."

"My dear Sancho, don't tell me you lay awake all night long?"

"Not all night long, of course. But far too much of it. You know well enough what I was up to."

"I don't *know* anything."

"I told you clearly enough. Before you went to bed."

"Ah but Sancho, I'm trained to forget what I'm told."

"It wasn't in the confessional."

"No, but it's very much easier if one is a priest to treat anything one is told as a confession. I never repeat what anybody tells me—even to myself if possible."

Sancho grunted and fell silent. Father Quixote thought that he detected a sense of disappointment in his companion, and he felt a little guilty.

In a restaurant called the Valencia, off the Plaza Mayor, sitting in a little patio behind the bar and drinking a glass of white wine, he felt his high spirits begin to return. He had enjoyed the visit they had first paid to the house of Cervantes which had cost them fifty pesetas each (he wondered whether he might have enjoyed a free entry if he had given his name at the desk). Some of the furniture had actually belonged to the biographer; a letter in his own hand addressed to the king dealing with the tax on oil was hung on the white lime-washed wall which he could well imagine splashed with blood on that terrible night when the bleeding body of Don Gaspar de Ezpelata had been carried inside and Cervantes had been arrested on the false suspicion of having been an accomplice in his murder. "Of course he was let out on bail," Father Quixote told Sancho, "but think of going on with the Life of my ancestor under the weight of that threat. I sometimes wonder whether he had that night in mind when he wrote of how *your* ancestor, after he became governor of the island, ordered a youth to sleep a night in gaol and the youth replied, 'You haven't enough power to make me sleep in prison.' Perhaps those were the very words that the old man Cervantes used to the magistrate. 'Suppose you order me to prison and put me in chains and shut me in a cell, all the same if I don't wish to sleep, you haven't the power to make me.' "

"The Civil Guard today," Sancho said, "would know how to answer that. They would put you to sleep fast enough with one blow." He added with gloom, "I could do with some sleep."

"Ah, but your ancestor, Sancho, was a kindly man and he let the youth go. And the magistrate did the same with Cervantes."

Now in the patio, while the sunlight touched with gold the white wine in his glass, Father Quixote's thoughts returned to Marx. He said, "You know, I think my ancestor would have got on well with Marx. Poor Marx—he had his books of chivalry too that belonged to the past."

"Marx was looking to the future."

"Yes, but he was mourning all the time for the past—the past of his imagination. Listen to this, Sancho—" and Father Quixote took *The Communist Manifesto* out of his pocket. " 'The bourgeoisie has put an end to all feudal, patriarchal, idyllic relations. . . . It has drowned the most heavenly ecstasies of religious fervour, of chivalrous enthusiasm in the icy water of egotistical calculation.' Can't you hear the very voice of my ancestor mourning for lost days? I learnt his words by heart when I was a boy and I remember them, though a bit roughly, still. 'Now idleness triumphs over labour, vice over virtue, presumption over valour, and theory over the practice of arms, which only lived and flourished in the golden age of knights errant. Amadis of Gaul, Palmerin of England, Roland. . . .' And listen to *The Communist Manifesto* again—you can't deny that this man Marx was a true follower of my ancestor. 'All fixed, fast-frozen relations, with their chain of ancient and venerable prejudices and opinions, are swept away, all new-found ones become antiquated before they can ossify.' He was a true prophet, Sancho. He even foresaw Stalin. 'All that is solid melts into air, all that is holy is profaned. . . .' "

A man who was lunching in the little patio paused with a fork half raised to his lips. Then, as Sancho looked across the floor at him, he bowed his head and began again hurriedly to eat. Sancho said, "I wish you wouldn't read quite so loudly, father. You are intoning as though you were in church."

"There are many holy words written which are not in the Bible or the Fathers. Those words of Marx demand in a way to be intoned. 'Heavenly ecstasies of religious fervour . . . chivalrous enthusiasm.' "

"Franco is dead, father, but all the same do please show a bit of prudence. That man over there is listening to every word you say."

"Of course, like all the prophets, Marx does make mistakes. Even Saint Paul was liable to error."

"I don't like the man's briefcase. It's an official sort of

briefcase. I can smell the Secret Police from thirty meters away."

"Let me read you what I think is his biggest mistake. The origin of all the other mistakes to come."

"For God's sake, father, if you must read, read in a low voice."

To please the Mayor, Father Quixote almost whispered the words. Sancho had to lean close to him in order to hear, and they must have had the air of two conspirators. " 'The proletarian is without property; his relation to his wife and children has no longer anything in common with the bourgeois family relations; modern industrial labour has stripped him of every trace of national character.' Perhaps that seemed true when he wrote, Sancho, but surely the world has taken a very different route. Listen to this too: 'The modern labourer, instead of rising with the progress of industry, sinks deeper and deeper below the conditions of existence of his own class. He becomes a pauper.' You know, once some years ago I took a holiday with a friend, a priest—his name was . . . oh dear, how one forgets names after a glass or two of wine. He had a parish on the Costa Brava (it was when Rocinante was very young) and I saw the English paupers—so Marx calls them—lying in the sun on the beaches there. As for not having a national character they had forced the local people to open what they called fish-and-chip shops; otherwise they would have taken their custom elsewhere, perhaps to France or Portugal."

"Oh, the English," Sancho said, "forget the English— they never conform to any rules, not even of economics. The Russian proletariat are no longer paupers either. The world has learnt from Marx and Russia. The Russian proletariat have their holidays paid for them in the Crimea. It's just as good as the Costa Brava."

"The proletariat I saw on the Costa Brava were paying

for their own holidays. You have to look for the Third World, Sancho, to find any paupers now. But that's not because of the triumph of Communism. Don't you think it would have happened without Communism? Why, it was already beginning to happen when Marx wrote, but he didn't notice. So that's why Communism had to be spread by force—force not only against the bourgeoisie, force against the proletariat too. It was humanism, not Communism, which turned the pauper into the bourgeois, and behind humanism there's always the shadow of religion— the religion of Christ as well as the religion of Marx. We are all bourgeois today. Don't tell me that Brezhnev is not just as much a bourgeois as you and me. If the whole world becomes bourgeois, will it be so bad—except for dreamers like Marx and my ancestor?"

"You make the world of the future sound like Utopia, father."

"Oh no, humanism and religion have not done away with either nationalism or imperialism. It's those two that cause the wars. Wars are not merely for economic reasons—they come from the emotions of men, like love does, from the color of a skin or the accent of a voice. From unhappy memories too. That's why I'm glad to have the short memory of a priest."

"I never thought you occupied yourself with politics."

"Not 'occupied.' But you've been my friend a long time, Sancho, and I want to understand you. *Das Kapital* has always defeated me. This little book is different. It's the work of a good man. A man as good as you are—and just as mistaken."

"Time will show."

"Time can never show. Our lives are far too short."

The man with the briefcase had put down his knife and fork and was signaling for his bill. When it came he paid rapidly without paying attention to the details.

"Well," Father Quixote said, "you can breathe easily now, Sancho, the man has gone."

"Let us hope he doesn't come back with the police behind him. He looked very closely at your bib as he left."

Father Quixote felt that at last he could raise his voice and speak more freely. "Of course," he said, "perhaps because I read so much in Saint Francis de Sales and Saint John of the Cross I find poor Marx's occasional admiration for the bourgeois a little farfetched."

"Admiration of the bourgeois? What on earth do you mean?"

"Of course an economist is bound to see things in very material terms, and I admit that perhaps I dwell too much on the spiritual."

"But he hated the bourgeois."

"Oh, hatred we know is often the other side of love. Perhaps, poor man, he had been rejected by what he loved. Listen to this, Sancho. 'The bourgeoisie, during its rule of scarce one hundred years, has created more massive and more colossal production forces than have all the preceding generations together. Subjection of Nature's forces to man, machinery, application of chemistry to industry and agriculture, steam navigation, railways, electric telegraphs, clearing of whole continents for cultivation, canalization of rivers, whole populations conjured out of the ground. . . .' It makes one almost proud to be a bourgeois, doesn't it? What a magnificent colonial governor Marx would have made. If only Spain had produced a man like that, perhaps we would never have lost our empire. Poor man, he had to put up with an overcrowded lodging in a poor part of London, and borrow from his friends."

"You look at Marx from a strange angle, father."

"I was prejudiced against him—even though he did defend the monasteries—but I had never read this little book. A first reading is something special, like first love. I wish I could come on Saint Paul now by accident and read him for the first time. If only you would try the experiment, Sancho, with one of what you call my books of chivalry."

"I would find your taste as absurd as Cervantes found your ancestor's."

It was a friendly meal in spite of their dispute and after a second bottle of wine they agreed to take the road towards León and to leave it to a later decision—perhaps even a cast of the dice—whether they made for the east towards the Basque territory or for the west towards Galicia. They left the Valencia arm in arm, but as they made towards the spot where they had parked Rocinante, Father Quixote could feel a pressure on his arm.

"What is it, Sancho?"

"The secret policeman. He's following us now. Don't say anything. Take the first turning we come to."

"But Rocinante is up the street."

"He wants to get the number of our car."

"How can you possibly know that he's a secret policeman?"

"By his briefcase," Sancho said, and it was true that, after they had turned the first corner and Father Quixote took a look behind, the man was still there, carrying the dreadful insignia of his profession.

"Don't turn round again," Sancho said. "We must let him think that we don't know he is there."

"How are we going to escape him?"

"We'll find a bar and order a drink. He'll linger outside. We'll go out through the back and get a start on him. Then cut around to Rocinante."

"Suppose there isn't a back door?"

"We'll have to go on to another bar."

There was no back door. Sancho drank a brandy and Father Quixote prudently took a coffee. When they left the man was still there twenty yards down the street, looking in a shop window.

"He seems to be rather obvious for a secret policeman,"

Father Quixote said as they moved up the street towards another bar.

"One of their tricks," Sancho said. "He wants to make us nervous." He guided Father Quixote into a second bar and ordered a second brandy.

"If I have any more coffee," Father Quixote said, "I shan't sleep tonight."

"Have a tonic water."

"What's that?"

"A sort of mineral water with a bit of quinine in it."

"No alcohol?"

"No, no." The brandy was making Sancho bellicose. "I've a good mind to beat the fellow up, but he's probably armed."

"This tonic water is really delicious," Father Quixote said. "Why have I never had it before? I could almost give up wine. Do you think I can buy it in El Toboso?"

"I don't know. I doubt it. If he keeps his gun in his briefcase I might be able to knock him out before he draws it."

"Do you know—I think I'll have another bottle."

"I'm going to look for a back door," Sancho said, and Father Quixote found himself quite alone in the bar. It was the hour of siesta and one revolving fan in the ceiling hardly made the place any cooler—at regular intervals there came a whiff of cold and then a spell of even greater heat by contrast. Father Quixote drained his tonic and ordered a third quickly so as to drink it before Sancho returned.

A voice behind him whispered, "Monsignor." He turned. It was the man with the briefcase, a small lean man in a black suit and a black tie which matched the case he carried. He had dark penetrating eyes behind steel-rimmed glasses and thin lips tightly closed, and he might well have been, Father Quixote thought, the harbinger of an evil destiny, perhaps the Grand Inquisitor himself. If only Sancho would return.

"What do you want?" Father Quixote demanded in what he hoped would sound a strong defiant voice, but the bubbles of the tonic water betrayed him and he hiccupped.

"I want to speak to you alone."

"I am alone."

The man nodded at the back of the barman. He said, "This is serious. Impossible to speak to you here. Please go through that door at the back."

But there were two doors—he wished he knew through which one Sancho had gone. "On the right," the man directed. Father Quixote obeyed; there was a short passage and two other doors. "Through there. The first one."

Father Quixote found that he was in a lavatory. In the mirror by the washbasin he could see that his captor was fumbling at the latch of his briefcase. To take out a gun? Was he to be shot in the back of the neck? Hastily, too hastily, he began an act of contrition under his breath: "Oh God, I am sorry and beg pardon for all my shoes—"

"Monsignor."

"Yes, friend," Father Quixote replied to the image which he watched in the glass. If he was to be shot he preferred the back of the neck to the face, for the face in its way is the mirror image of God.

"I want you to hear my confession."

Father Quixote hiccupped. The door opened and Sancho peered in. "Father Quixote," he exclaimed.

"Go away," Father Quixote said. "I am hearing a confession."

He turned to the stranger and tried to regain the dignity of the cloth. "This is hardly a suitable place. Why have you chosen me and not your own priest?"

"I have just been burying him," the man said. "I am an   115 undertaker." He opened his briefcase and took out a large brass handle.

Father Quixote said, "I am not in my diocese. I have no faculty here."

"A monsignor is free from such rules. When I saw you in the restaurant I thought, 'Here is my chance.' "

Father Quixote said, "I'm a very new monsignor. Are you sure about the rules?"

"Anyway, in an emergency any priest. . . . This is an emergency."

"But there are many priests in Valladolid. Go to any church."

"I could see from your eyes that you were a priest who would understand."

"Understand what?"

The man began quickly to mumble the act of contrition, but at least he got the words right. Father Quixote felt himself at a loss. Never before had he heard a confession in such surroundings. He had always been seated in that box like a coffin. . . . It was almost automatically that he took refuge in the only box available and sat down on a closed lavatory seat. The stranger would have got down on his knees, but Father Quixote stopped him, for the floor was not at all clean. "Don't kneel," he said. "Just stand as you are." The man held out the large brass handle. He said, "I have sinned and I ask the forgiveness of God through you, father. I mean monsignor."

"I'm not a monsignor in this box," Father Quixote said. "There are no ranks in the confessional. What have you done?"

"I have stolen this handle and another handle like it."

"Then you must give them back."

"The owner is dead. I buried him this morning."

Father Quixote shielded his eyes with a hand, as the custom is, for the sake of secrecy, but a vision of the dark vulpine face remained clearly in his mind. He was a priest who liked to hear a quick confession in the simple abstract words that penitents usually employed. They seldom entailed more than one simple question—how many times . . . ? I have committed adultery, I have neglected my Easter duties, I have sinned against purity. . . . He was not used to a sin in the form of a brass handle. Surely a handle like that could have little value.

"You should return the handle to the heirs."

"Father Gonzalez left no heirs."

"But what are these handles? When did you steal them?"

"I charged for them in my bill and then I took them off the coffin so that I could use them again."

"Do you often do that?" Father Quixote could not restrain the fatal curiosity which was his recurring fault in the confessional.

"Oh, it's a common practice. All my competitors do it."

Father Quixote wondered what Father Heribert Jone would have written about this case. He would certainly list it among sins against justice, the category to which adultery also belongs, but Father Quixote seemed to remember that in the case of theft the gravity of the sin had to be judged by the value of the object stolen—if it was equivalent to one seventh of the owner's monthly wage it must be treated seriously. If the owner were a millionaire there would be no sin at all—at least not against justice. What would Father Gonzalez have earned monthly and indeed was he the true owner if he had only come into possession of the handles after death? A coffin surely belonged only to the earth in which it was laid.

He asked—more to allow himself time to think than for any other reason—"Have you confessed to the other occasions?"

"No. I told you, monsignor, it is a recognized practice in my profession. We charge extra for brass handles, that's true, but it's only a kind of rent. Till the interment is over."

"Then why are you confessing to me now?"

"Perhaps I am a too scrupulous man, monsignor, but it seemed somehow different when I buried Father Gonzalez. He would have been so proud of the brass handles. You see, it showed how esteemed he was in the parish, because, naturally, it was the parish which paid."

"And you contributed?"

"Oh yes. Of course. I was very fond of Father Gonzalez."

"So in a way you were stealing from yourself?"

"Not stealing, monsignor."

"I've told you not to call me monsignor. You say that you have not stolen, that it is the practice of your colleagues to remove these handles. . . ."

"Yes."

"Then what is troubling your conscience?"

The man gave a gesture which could have been one of bewilderment. Father Quixote thought: How many times I have felt guilty as he does without knowing why. Sometimes he envied the certitude of those who were able to lay down clear rules—Father Heribert Jone, his bishop, even the Pope. Himself, he lived in a mist, unable to see a path, stumbling. He said, "Don't worry about such little things. Go home and have a good sleep. Perhaps you have stolen. . . . Do you think God cares so much about a small thing like that? He has created a universe—we don't know how many stars and planets and worlds. You have stolen two brass handles—don't feel so important. Say you are sorry for your pride and go home."

The man said, "But please—my absolution."

Father Quixote unwillingly muttered the unnecessary formula. The man put the handle back in the briefcase, closed it, and made a kind of duck in the direction of Father Quixote before he went out. Father Quixote sat on the lavatory seat with a sense of exhaustion and inadequacy. He thought: I didn't say the right words. Why do I never find the right words? The man needed help and I recited a formula. God forgive me. Will someone only give me a formula too when I come to die?

After a while he went back into the bar. Sancho was there waiting for him and drinking another brandy.

"What on earth have you been up to?"

"Practicing my profession," Father Quixote replied.

"In a lavatory?"

"In a lavatory, in a prison, in a church. What's the difference?"

"You got rid of that man?"

Father Quixote said, "I suppose I did. I'm a bit tired, Sancho. I know it's extravagant, but could I have just one more bottle of tonic water?"

IX

HOW MONSIGNOR QUIXOTE SAW A STRANGE SPECTACLE

Their stay in Valladolid was unexpectedly prolonged by a firm reluctance on the part of Rocinante to take the road again, so she had to be left in a garage for examination.

"Little wonder," Father Quixote said. "Yesterday the poor thing covered an immense distance."

"An immense distance! We are less than one hundred and twenty kilometers from Salamanca."

"Her usual stint is ten—when I have to fetch wine from the cooperative."

"It's just as well then that we decided against Rome or Moscow. If you want my opinion you have spoilt her. Cars, like women, should never be spoilt."

"But she's very old, Sancho. Older than we are probably. After all—without her help. . . . Could we have walked all the way from Salamanca?"

As they had to wait for the verdict on Rocinante until the morning, Sancho suggested that they might visit a cinema. Father Quixote agreed after some hesitation. There had once been a period when stage plays were forbidden to the priesthood, and though the regulation had never applied to the cinema, which had not then existed, there remained in Father Quixote's mind a sensation of something dangerous
120   about a spectacle.

"I have never been to a cinema before," he told Sancho.

"You must know the world if you are to convert the world," Sancho said.

"You will not think me a hypocrite," Father Quixote asked, "if I remove what you call my bib?"

"All colors are the same in the dark," Sancho said, "but do as you like."

Father Quixote on second thoughts left his *pechera* on. It seemed more honest. He didn't wish to be accused of hypocrisy.

They went to a small cinema which advertised a film called *A Maiden's Prayer*. The title had attracted Father Quixote just as much as it repelled Sancho, who foresaw an evening of boredom and piety. However, he was mistaken. The film was no masterpiece, but all the same he found it quite enjoyable though he was a little afraid of how Father Quixote would react, for the film was certainly not maidenly, and he should have noticed that the poster outside was marked with a warning "S."

In fact the maiden's prayer turned out to be a very handsome young man whose adventures with a series of young girls ended always, with the monotony of repetition, in bed. The photography at that point became soft and confusing, and it was a little bit difficult to discern whose legs belonged to whom since the private parts, which distinguish a man from a woman, were skillfully avoided by the camera. Was it the man or the girl who was on top? Whose parts were being kissed by whom? On these occasions there was no dialogue to help the viewer: only the sound of hard breathing and sometimes a grunt or a squeal, which could be either masculine or feminine. To make things even more difficult the scenes had obviously been shot for a small screen (perhaps for a home movie) and the images became still more abstract when enlarged for a cinema. Even Sancho's enjoyment waned: he would have much preferred more overt pornography, and it was difficult to identify with the principal actor who had very shiny black hair and side whiskers. Sancho thought that he recognized the model who had appeared frequently on television for a male deodorant.

The end of the film was certainly an anticlimax. The young man had fallen deeply in love with the one girl who had resisted his advances. There was a church wedding, a chaste kiss at the altar when the bridegroom slipped the ring on the bride's finger, and then a quick cut to a tangle of limbs in bed—it occurred to Sancho that for the sake of economy they had simply repeated one of the earlier scenes with the anonymous limbs, or was it perhaps a touch of intelligent irony on the part of the director? The lights went on and Father Quixote said, "How very interesting, Sancho. So that's what they call a film."

"It wasn't a very good example."

"What a lot of exercise they were all taking. The actors must be quite exhausted."

"They were only simulating, father."

"How do you mean, simulating? What were they pretending to do?"

"To make love of course."

"Oh, so that's how it's done. I always imagined it to be a great deal more simple and more enjoyable. They seemed to suffer such a lot. From the sounds they made."

"They were pretending—this is acting, father—to have unbearable pleasure."

"They didn't seem to find it pleasurable—or perhaps they were bad actors. They just went on suffering. And I saw no balloons, Sancho."

"I was afraid you might be shocked, father, but it was you who chose the film."

"Yes. By the title. But I don't understand what the title had to do with what we saw."

"Well, I suppose that a maiden's prayer is to find a handsome young man to love."

"That word 'love' again. I don't believe that Señorita Martin prayed for anything like that. But all the same I was impressed by the silence of the audience. They took it so seriously that I was really afraid to laugh."

"You wanted to laugh?"

"Yes. It was difficult not to. But I don't like to offend anyone who takes a thing seriously. Laughter is not an argument. It can be a stupid abuse. Perhaps they saw things differently from me. Perhaps it was beauty that they saw. All the same, sometimes I longed for one of them to laugh —even you, Sancho—so that I could laugh too. But I was afraid to break that total silence. There is something holy in silence. It would hurt me if in church when I raised the Host someone laughed."

"Suppose everyone in the church laughed?"

"Ah, that would be quite different. Then I would think —I might be wrong of course—that I was hearing the laughter of joy. A solitary laugh is so often a laugh of superiority."

That night in bed Father Quixote opened his volume of Saint Francis de Sales. He still found himself worried by those scenes of love-making in the cinema—worried by his failure to be moved by any emotion except amusement. He had always believed that human love was the same in kind as the love of God, even though only the faintest and feeblest reflection of that love, but those exercises which had made him want to laugh aloud, those grunts and squeals. . . . Am I, he wondered, incapable of feeling human love? For, if I am, then I must also be incapable of feeling love for God. He began to fear that his spirit might be stamped indelibly by that terrible question mark. He desperately wanted comfort and so he turned to what Sancho had called his books of chivalry, but he couldn't help remembering that Don Quixote at the last had renounced them on his deathbed. Perhaps he too when the end arrived. . . .

He opened *The Love of God* at random, but the *sortes*   123

Virgilianae gave him no comfort. He tried three times and then he struck a passage which did seem relevant to what he had seen in the cinema. Not that it made him happier, for it made him think that perhaps he had even less capacity to love than a piece of iron. "Iron has such a sympathy with Adamant that as soon as it is touched with the virtue thereof it turns towards it, it begins to stir and quiver with a little hopping, testifying in that the complacence it takes, and thereupon it doth advance and bear itself towards the Adamant, striving by all means possible to be united to it." And then came a question which pierced him to the heart. "And do you not see all the parts of a lively love represented in this lifeless stone?" Oh yes, he had seen a great deal of hopping, he thought, but he had not experienced the lively love.

The dreaded question mark was still stamped on his spirit when they set out next day. Rocinante was positively skittish after her stay in the garage and complained not at all when their speed mounted to forty—even forty-five—kilometers an hour, a speed which they only attained because Father Quixote was deep in his unhappy thoughts. "What is wrong?" Sancho asked him. "Again today you are the Monsignor of the Sorrowful Countenance."

"I have sometimes thought, may God forgive me," Father Quixote said, "that I was specially favored because I have never been troubled with sexual desires."

"Not even in dreams?"

"No, not even in dreams."

"You are a very lucky man."

Am I? he questioned himself. Or am I the most unfortunate? He couldn't say to the friend who sat beside him what he was thinking—the question he was asking himself. How can I pray to resist evil when I am not even tempted? There is no virtue in such a prayer. He felt completely alone in his silence. It was as though the area of the confessional box and the secrets which it held had extended beyond the box itself and beyond the penitent to include the car he sat in, even the wheel under his hand as they drove towards León. He prayed in his silence: O God, make me human, let me feel temptation. Save me from my indifference.

X

HOW MONSIGNOR QUIXOTE CONFRONTED JUSTICE

1

They stopped on their way to León in a field on a river bank near the village of Mansilla de las Mulas because the Mayor claimed to have a great thirst. A small footbridge gave them a shadow in which they could leave the car, but in fact Sancho's thirst was only a subterfuge to break the silence of Father Quixote which was getting badly on his nerves. A drink might unlock Father Quixote's mouth, and he lowered a bottle of their Manchegan wine into the river on a string, awaking the interest of some cows on the other bank. He came back to find Father Quixote staring gloomily down at his purple socks, and he could bear the inexplicable silence no longer. He said, "For God's sake, if you have taken a vow of silence go into a monastery. There are Carthusians at Burgos and Trappists at Osera. Take your choice, monsignor, which way we go."

"I am sorry, Sancho," Father Quixote said. "It's only my thoughts. . . ."

"Oh, I suppose your thoughts are too high and spiritual for a mere Marxist to understand them."

"No, no."

"Remember, father, what a good governor my ancestor made. Don Quixote with all his chivalry and courage would never have governed so well. What a holy mess—I *mean* a holy mess—he would have made of that island. My ancestor took to governing just as Trotsky took to commanding an army. Trotsky was without experience, and yet he beat the White generals. Oh, we are materialists, I know, peasants and Marxists. But don't despise us for that."

"When have I ever despised you, Sancho?"

"Oh well, thank your God that you've begun to speak again. Let's open the bottle."

The wine he fished from the river was not quite cold enough, but he was anxious to complete the cure. They drank two glasses in what was now a friendly silence.

"Is there any cheese left, father?"

"I think a little. I'll go and see."

Father Quixote was gone a long time. Perhaps the cheese had been hard to find. The Mayor got impatiently up as Father Quixote came out from under the bridge with a look of justifiable anxiety on his face, for he was accompanied by a Guardia. For a reason the Mayor could not understand he was talking rapidly to his companion in Latin and the Guardia too had a look of anxiety. Father Quixote said, *"Esto mihi in Deum protectorem et in locum refugii."*

"The bishop seems to be a foreigner," the Guardia told the Mayor.

"He is not a bishop. He is a monsignor."

"Is that your car under the bridge?"

"It belongs to the monsignor."

"I told him he should have locked it. Why, he had even left his key in the starter. It's not a safe thing to do. Not around here."

"It seems very peaceful here. Even the cows. . . ."

"You haven't seen a man with a bullet hole through his right trouser leg and a false moustache? Though I expect he has thrown that away."

"No, no. Nothing of the kind."

"*Scio cui credidi*," Father Quixote said.

"Italian?" the Guardia asked. "The Pope's a great Pope."

"He certainly is."

"No hat or jacket. A striped shirt."

"No one like that has been around here."

"He got that bullet hole in Zamora. Narrow escape. One of ours. How long have you been here?"

"About a quarter of an hour."

"Coming from where?"

"Valladolid."

"Not passed anyone on the road?"

"No."

"He can't have got much farther than this in the time."

"What's he done?"

"He robbed a bank at Benavente. Shot the cashier. Escaped on a Honda. Found abandoned—the Honda, I mean—five kilometers away. That's why it's not safe leaving your car unlocked like that with the key in the starter."

"*Laqueus contritus est*," Father Quixote said, "*et nos liberati sumus.*"

"What's the monsignor saying?"

The Mayor said, "I'm not a linguist myself."

"You are on the way to León?"

"Yes."

"Keep an eye open and don't give a lift to any stranger." He saluted the monsignor with courtesy and a certain caution and left them.

"Why were you talking Latin to him?" the Mayor asked.

"It seemed a good thing to do."

"But why . . . ?"

"I wanted if possible to avoid a lie," Father Quixote replied. "Even an officious lie, not a malicious one, to use the distinction made by Father Heribert Jone."

"What had you got to lie about?"

"I was confronted very suddenly with the possibility— you might say the temptation."

The Mayor sighed. Father Quixote's silence had certainly been broken by the wine and he almost regretted it. He said, "Did you find any cheese?"

"I found a quite substantial piece, but I gave it to him."

"The Guardia? Why on earth—?"

"No, no, the man he was looking for, of course."

"You mean you've *seen* the man?"

"Oh yes, that was why I was afraid of questions."

"For God's sake, where is he now?"

"In the boot of the car. It was careless of me, after that, as the Guardia said, to leave the key. . . . Somebody might have driven away with him. Oh well, the danger is over now."

For a long moment the Mayor was incapable of speech. Then he said, "What did you do with the wine?"

"Together we put it on the back seat of the car."

"I thank God," the Mayor said, "that I had the number plate changed at Valladolid."

"What do you mean, Sancho?"

"Those Civil Guards will have reported your number at Avila. They'll be on a computer by this time."

"But my papers. . . ."

"You've got new ones. Of course it took time. That's why we stayed so long in Valladolid. The garagist there is an old friend and a member of the Party."

"Sancho, Sancho, how many years in prison have we earned?"

"Not half as many as you will get for hiding a fugitive from justice. Whatever induced you . . . ?"

"He asked me to help him. He said he was falsely accused and confused with another man."

"With a revolver hole in his trousers? A bank robber?"

"Well, so was your leader, Stalin. So much depends on motive, after all. If Stalin had come to me in confession and explained his reasons honestly I would have given him perhaps a decade of the rosary to say, though I've never given so severe a penance to anyone in El Toboso. You remember what my ancestor told the galley-slaves before he released them, 'There is a God in heaven, who does not neglect to punish the wicked nor to reward the good, and it is not right that honorable men should be executioners of others.' That's good Christian doctrine, Sancho. A decade of the rosary—it's severe enough. We are not executioners or interrogators. The Good Samaritan didn't hold an enquiry into the wounded man's past—the man who had fallen among thieves—before he helped him. Perhaps he was a publican and the thieves were only taking back what he had taken from them."

"While you are talking, monsignor, our wounded man is probably dying for lack of air."

They hurried to the car and found the man in a grievous enough state. The false moustache, loosened by sweat, hung down from one corner of his upper lip. It was lucky for him that he was small and had folded fairly easily into the little space which Rocinante offered.

All the same he complained bitterly when they let him out. "I thought I was going to die. What kept you so long?"

"We were doing our best for you," Father Quixote said in much the same words as his ancestor had used. "We are not your judges, but your conscience should tell you that ingratitude is an ignoble sin."

"We've done a great deal too much for you," Sancho said. "Now be off. The Guardia went that way. I would advise you to keep to the fields until you can drown yourself in the city."

"How can I keep to the fields in these shoes which are rotten from the soles up and how can I drown myself in the city with a revolver hole in my trousers?"

"You robbed the bank. You can buy yourself a new pair of shoes."

"Who said I robbed a bank?" He pulled out his empty pockets. "Search me," he said. "You call yourselves Christians."

"I don't," the Mayor said. "I am a Marxist."

"I've got a pain in my back. I can't walk a step."

"I've got some aspirin in the car," Father Quixote said. He unlocked the car and began to look in the glove compartment. Behind him he heard a cough twice repeated. "I have some lozenges too," he said. "I suppose there was a draught in the boot." He turned with the medicine in his hand and saw to his surprise that the stranger was holding a revolver. "You mustn't point a thing like that," he said, "it's dangerous."

"What size shoe do you take?" the man demanded.

"I really forget. I think thirty-nine."

"And you?"

"Forty," Sancho said.

"Give me yours," the man commanded Father Quixote.

"They are nearly as rotten as your own."

"Don't argue. I'd take your pants too if they would only fit. Now both of you turn your backs. If one of you moves I shall shoot both."

Father Quixote said, "I don't understand why you went to rob a bank—if that's what you were doing—in a pair of rotten shoes."

"I took the wrong pair by mistake. That's why. You can turn round now. Get back into the car, both of you. I'll sit at the back and if you stop anywhere for any reason I shall shoot."

"Where do you want to go?" Sancho asked.

"You will drop me by the cathedral in León."

Father Quixote reversed out of the field with some difficulty.

"You are a very bad driver," the man said.

"It's Rocinante. She never likes going backwards. I'm 131

afraid you haven't much room there with all that wine. Shall I stop and return the case to the boot?"

"No. Go on."

"Whatever happened to your Honda? The Guardia said you abandoned it."

"I ran out of petrol. I had forgotten to fill the tank."

"Wrong pair of shoes. No petrol. It really does look as though God was against your plans."

"Can't you drive any quicker?"

"No. Rocinante is very old. She is apt to break down at over forty." He looked in the driving-mirror and saw the revolver pointing at him. "I wish you would relax and put the gun down," he said. "Rocinante sometimes behaves a bit like a camel. If she shakes you up suddenly that thing might go off. You wouldn't be very happy with another man's death on your conscience."

"What do you mean? Another man?"

"The poor fellow in the bank whom you killed."

"I didn't kill him. I missed."

"God does certainly seem to have been working over-time," Father Quixote said, "to preserve you from grave sin."

"Anyway it wasn't a bank. It was a self-service store."

"The Guardia said a bank."

"Oh, they would say it was a bank even if it was a public lavatory. They feel more important that way."

As they entered the city Father Quixote noticed that the gun always disappeared from view when they stopped at traffic lights. He could perhaps have jumped out of the car, but that would have left Sancho in danger, and if he tempted the man to further violence he would be sharing his sin. In any case he had no wish to be an instrument of human justice. It was a great relief when they met no Guardia or *Carabiñero* before they drew up as close to the cathedral as he could get. "Let me look around and see that it is safe," he said.

"If you betray me," the man said, "I will shoot your friend."

Father Quixote opened the door. "All's well," he said. "You can go."

"If you are lying," the man warned him, "the first bullet's for you."

"Your moustache has fallen off," Father Quixote told him. "It's stuck to your shoe—I mean my shoe."

They watched the man out of sight.

"At least he didn't assault me like the galley-slaves assaulted my forebear," Father Quixote said.

"Stay in the car while I go and buy you some shoes. You said size thirty-nine?"

"Would you mind if we went into the cathedral first? It's been rather a strain, keeping Rocinante from bucking. If he had killed us the poor man would have been in really serious trouble. I would like to sit down just for a little in the cool—and to pray. I won't keep you long."

"I thought you were doing a lot of that while you drove."

"Oh yes, I was—but those were prayers for the poor man. I'd like to thank God now for *our* safety."

The stone struck cold through his purple socks. He regretted that in Salamanca he had not chosen the woolen ones. He was dwarfed by the great height of the nave and the flood of light through a hundred and twenty windows which might have been the gaze of God. He felt as though he were an infinitely small creature set on the slide of a microscope. He escaped to a side altar and knelt down. He didn't know what to say. When he thought "Thank you," the words seemed as hollow as an echo—he felt no gratitude for his escape; perhaps he would have been able to feel a little gratitude if a bullet had struck him— this is the end. They would have taken his body back to El Toboso and there he would have been at home again and not on this absurd pilgrimage—to what? Or where?

It seemed a waste of time trying and failing to pray, so he gave up the attempt and instead tried to exclude all thought, to be aware of nothing, to enter a complete silence, and after a long while he did feel himself on the threshold of Nothing with only one step to take. Then he became aware of his left big toe colder than the other on the cathedral stone, and he thought: I have a hole in my sock. The sock—why had he not insisted on wool?—was not worth the price at that grand establishment patronized by Opus Dei.

He made the sign of the cross and rejoined Sancho.

"Have you prayed enough?" the Mayor asked him.

"I haven't prayed at all."

They left Rocinante parked and walked at random through the streets. Just off the Burgo Nuevo they found a shoe shop. The hot pavements burnt Father Quixote's feet and the hole from which his left big toe protruded grew considerably larger. It was a small shop and the proprietor looked at his feet with astonishment.

"I want a pair of black shoes, size thirty-nine," Father Quixote said.

"Yes, yes, please take a seat." The man produced a pair and knelt before him. Father Quixote thought: I am like the statue of Saint Peter in Rome. Will he kiss my toe? He laughed.

"What's funny?" the Mayor asked.

"Oh nothing, nothing. A thought."

"You will find the leather of this pair very soft and supple, Your Excellency."

"I am not a bishop," Father Quixote said, "only a monsignor and God forgive me for that."

The man fitted the shoe over the undamaged sock. "If the monsignor would just take a few steps. . . ."

"I've taken more than a few steps in León already. Your pavements are hard."

134

"Certainly they must have been, monsignor, walking without shoes."

"These shoes are very comfortable. I will take them."

"Would you like them wrapped or will you wear them, monsignor?"

"Of course I will wear them. Do you think I *want* to walk barefoot?"

"I thought perhaps. . . . Well, I thought, maybe it was a penance. . . ."

"No, no, I am not, I fear, a holy man."

He sat down again and let the man fit the other shoe over the protruding toe which he adjusted with gentleness and even a touch of reverence, pushing it back into the sock. It was obvious that to be in contact with a monsignor's naked toe was a new experience for him.

"And the other shoes? The monsignor does not require them wrapped?"

"What other shoes?"

"The ones that monsignor has discarded."

"I didn't discard them. They discarded me," Father Quixote said. "I don't even know where they are. Far away from here, I expect, by this time. They were old shoes anyway. Not so good as these."

The man saw them to the shop door. He asked, "If you would give me your blessing, monsignor?" Father Quixote sketched the sign of the cross and mumbled. In the street he commented, "The man was far too respectful for my liking."

"The circumstances were not normal, and I'm afraid he is likely to remember us."

On the way back to Rocinante they passed a post office. Father Quixote halted. He said, "I am anxious."

"You have reason. If that scoundrel you saved is caught and talks. . . ."

"I was not thinking of him. I was thinking of Teresa. I   135 can feel in my head like a thunderstorm that something is wrong. We have been away such a long time."

"Four days."

"It's not possible. It seems a month at least. Please let me telephone."

"Go ahead, but be quick about it. The sooner we are out of León the better."

Teresa answered the telephone. Before he had time to speak she said in a tone of fury, "Father Herrera is not here and I don't know when he will return." She cut the line.

"Something *is* wrong," Father Quixote said. He dialed again and this time he spoke at once. "This is Father Quixote, Teresa."

"Praise be to God," Teresa said. "Where are you?"

"León."

"Where's that?"

The Mayor said, "You shouldn't have told her."

"What are you doing there, father?"

"Telephoning to you."

"Father, the bishop is in a terrible state."

"Is he ill, poor man?"

"He's in a holy rage."

"What's wrong, Teresa?"

"He's been on the telephone twice to Father Herrera. Half an hour it was they were talking, both times with no thought of expense."

"But what about, Teresa?"

"About you, of course. They say you are mad. They say you should be shut in a madhouse to save the honor of the Church."

"But why? Why?"

"The Guardia have been searching for you in Avila."

"I haven't been in Avila."

"They know that. They say you are in Valladolid. And

they say you exchanged clothes with the Red Mayor to escape."

"It's not true."

"They think you may be mixed up with those mad Basques."

"How do you know all this, Teresa?"

"Do you think I'd let them use your telephone and not leave the kitchen door open?"

"Let me speak to Father Herrera."

"Give nothing away," Sancho said. "Nothing."

"Father Herrera is not here. He left yesterday before it was light to see the bishop. The bishop's in such a fetch it wouldn't surprise me if he telephoned to the Holy Father himself about you. Father Herrera said to me it was a terrible mistake that the Holy Father made appointing you a monsignor. I said to him that's blasphemy. The Holy Father can't make mistakes."

"Oh yes, he can, Teresa—little mistakes. I think I'd better come home at once."

"You can't do that, father. The Guardia will grab you for sure and you'll end your days in the madhouse."

"But I'm no more mad than Father Herrera is. Or the bishop, come to that."

"They'll pretend you are. I heard Father Herrera say to the bishop, 'He's got to be kept out of mischief. For the sake of the Church.' Stay away, father."

"Goodbye, Teresa."

"You will stay away?"

"I must think about it, Teresa."

Father Quixote said to the Mayor, "The Guardia have been in touch with the bishop and the bishop with Father Herrera. They think I'm mad."

"Well there's no harm in that. They thought your ancestor was mad too. Perhaps Father Herrera will behave like the canon and start burning your books."

"God forbid. I ought to go home, Sancho."

"That would prove you mad indeed. We have to get away from here quickly but not to El Toboso. You should never have told Teresa that you were in León."

"She has a mouth like a padlock. Don't worry. Why, she never even told me about the horse steaks."

"There's a lot else to worry about. These computers work like lightning. They may be confused for a while by the change in the number plate, but if the Guardia have fed your title into the machine, we are in for trouble. We'll have to take off your bib and your socks again. I don't suppose there are many monsignors driving around in an old Seat 600."

As they walked rapidly away to where they had parked Rocinante, Sancho said, "I think we should abandon the car and take a bus."

"We've done nothing wrong."

"The danger is not what we have done, but what they think we have done. Even if it's no longer a crime to read Marx it's still a crime to hide a bank robber."

"He was not a bank robber."

"A self-service-store robber then—it's a crime to hide him in the boot of your car."

"I won't abandon Rocinante." They had reached the car and he put his hand protectively on the wing where he could feel a dent which had been caused when he scraped once against the butcher's car in El Toboso. "Do you know Shakespeare's play *Henry VIII?*"

"No, I much prefer Lope de Vega."

"I wouldn't like Rocinante to reproach me as Cardinal Wolsey did his king.

> Had I but serv'd my God with half the zeal
> I serv'd my king he would not in my age
> Have left me naked to mine enemies.

You see this bruise on her bonnet, Sancho? It was seven years ago and more that she suffered it through my fault. *Mea culpa, mea culpa, mea maxima culpa.*"

2

They drove out of León the quickest way, but as the road climbed Rocinante showed signs of fatigue. The mountains of León rose before them, gray, stony, jagged. The Mayor said, "You told me you wanted silence. The time has come to choose between the silence of Burgos and the silence of Osera."

"Burgos is a place of unhappy associations."

"Bravo, monsignor, I had thought the memory of the Generalissimo's headquarters might have attracted you."

"I prefer the silence of peace to the silence which comes after success—that silence is like the permanent silence of death. And not a good death either. But you, Sancho— doesn't the thought of a monastery repel you?"

"Why should it? They can defend us against worse evils, as Marx wrote. Besides, a monastery has the same advantage for us as a brothel. If we don't stay too long. There are no forms to fill up."

"Osera then, Sancho, and the Trappists."

"We shall at least have good Galician wine there. Our Manchegan will soon be running low."

They picnicked on wine only, for the cheese was gone with the robber and the sausage was finished. They were nearly a thousand meters up and the whole empty landscape lay below them, and a small wind freshened the air. They finished a bottle quickly and Sancho opened another. "Is that wise?" Father Quixote asked.

"Wisdom is not absolute," Sancho said. "Wisdom is relative to a given situation. Wisdom too varies with the individual case. For me it is wise to drink another half bottle in a situation like ours when we have no food. For you of course it may well be folly. In that case, when the time comes, I shall have to judge what it is wise for me to do with your half of the bottle."

"That time is unlikely to come," Father Quixote said. "In my wisdom I must prevent you drinking more than your share," and he poured himself out a glass. He added, "I don't understand why our lack of food can affect the wisdom of our choice."

"It is obvious," Sancho said. "Wine contains sugar and sugar is a very valuable food."

"In that case, if we had enough wine we should never starve."

"Exactly, but there is always a fallacy to be found in a logical argument—even in those of your Saint Thomas Aquinas. If we substituted wine for food we should have to stay where we are and so we would eventually run out of wine."

"Why would we have to stay?"

"Because neither of us would be capable of driving."

"True enough. Logical thought does often lead to absurd situations. There is a popular saint in La Mancha who lost her virginity when she was raped by a Moor in her own kitchen when he was unarmed and she had a kitchen knife in her hand."

"She wanted to be raped, I suppose."

"No, no, her thought was quite logical. Her virginity was less important than the salvation of the Moor. By killing him at that moment she was robbing him of any chance of salvation. An absurd and yet, when one thinks of it, a beautiful story."

"This wine is making you talkative, monsignor. I wonder
140 how you will put up with silence in the monastery."

"We shall not have to be silent, Sancho, and the monks have permission to speak to their guests."

"How quickly this second bottle has vanished. Do you remember—what a long time ago it seems—how you tried to explain the Trinity to me?"

"Yes. And I made that terrible mistake. I allowed a half bottle to represent the Holy Ghost."

"We won't make that mistake again," Sancho said as he opened a third bottle.

Father Quixote made no protest, and yet the wine was working in his brain like an irritant. He was ready to take offense as soon as an opportunity arose.

"I am glad," the Mayor said, "that unlike your ancestor you enjoy your wine. Don Quixote frequently stopped at an inn, he had at least four of his adventures at an inn, but we never hear of him drinking so much as a glass. Like us he had many meals of cheese in the open air but never a glass of good Manchegan to wash it down. As a travel companion he wouldn't have suited me. Thank God, in spite of your saintly books, you can drink deep when you choose."

"Why are you always saddling me with my ancestor?"

"I was only comparing—"

"You talk about him at every opportunity, you pretend that my saints' books are like his books of chivalry, you compare our little adventures with his. Those Guardia were Guardia, not windmills. I am Father Quixote, and not Don Quixote. I tell you, I exist. My adventures are my own adventures, not his. I go my way—my way—not his. I have free will. I am not tethered to an ancestor who has been dead these four hundred years."

"I am sorry, father. I thought you were proud of your ancestor. I never meant to offend."

"Oh, I know what you think. You think my God is an illusion like the windmills. But He exists, I tell you. I don't just believe in Him. I touch Him."

"Is he soft or hard?"

Father Quixote began to raise himself in wrath from the grass.

"No, no, father. I'm sorry. I didn't mean to joke. I respect your belief as you respect mine. Only there's a difference. I *know* that Marx and Lenin existed. You only believe."

"I tell you it's not a question of belief. I touch Him."

"Father, we've had a good time together. This is the third bottle. I raise my glass in honor of the Trinity. You can't refuse to drink that toast with me."

Father Quixote stared glumly into his glass. "No, I can't refuse, but. . . ." He drank and this time he felt his anger dissipate and in place of the anger a great sadness grew. He said, "Do you think that I am a little drunk, Sancho?" Sancho saw tears in his eyes.

"Father, our friendship. . . ."

"Yes, yes, nothing can alter that, Sancho. I only wish I had the right words."

"For what?"

"And the learning too. I am a very ignorant man. There was so much that I was supposed to teach in El Toboso that I didn't understand. I didn't think twice about it. The Trinity. Natural Law. Mortal sin. I taught them words out of textbooks. I never said to myself, do I believe these things? I went home and read my saints. They wrote of love. I could understand that. The other things didn't seem important."

"I don't understand what worries you, father."

"You worry me, Sancho. Four days of your company worry me. I think of myself laughing when I blew up that balloon. That film. . . . Why wasn't I shocked? Why didn't I walk out? El Toboso seems a hundred years away. I don't feel myself at all, Sancho. There's a giddiness. . . ."

"You *are* a little drunk, father. That's all."

"Are these the usual symptoms?"

"Talking a lot . . . giddiness . . . yes."

"And sadness?"

"It takes some people that way. Others become noisy and gay."

"I think I shall have to stick to tonic water. I don't feel up to driving."

"I could take the wheel."

"Rocinante doesn't like a strange hand. I would like to sleep for a little now before we go on. If I've said anything to offend you, Sancho, forgive me. It was the wine that spoke, not me."

"You've said nothing bad. Lie down for a while, father, and I'll keep watch. Vodka has given me a good head."

Father Quixote found a patch of soft turf between the rocks and lay down, but sleep did not come immediately. He said, "Father Heribert Jone found drunkenness a more serious sin than gluttony. I don't understand that. A little drunkenness has brought us together, Sancho. It helps friendship. Gluttony surely is a solitary vice. A form of onanism. And yet I remember Father Jone writing that it is only a venial sin, 'even if vomiting is produced.' Those are his very words."

"I wouldn't accept Father Jone as an authority on morals any more than I would accept Trotsky as an authority on Communism."

"Do people really do terrible things when they are drunk?"

"Perhaps, sometimes, if they lose control. But that's not always bad. It's good to lose control on occasions. In love, for example."

"Like those people in the film?"

"Well, yes, perhaps."

"Perhaps if they had drunk a little more they would have been blowing up balloons."

An odd sound came from the rocks. It took a moment

for the Mayor to recognize it as a laugh. Father Quixote said, "You are my moral theologian, Sancho," and a moment later a light snore took the place of the laugh.

3

It had been a tiring day, they had drunk well, and after a little while the Mayor too slept. He had a dream—it was one of those final dreams one has before waking of which even the small details stay hauntingly in the memory. He was searching for Father Quixote, who was lost. The Mayor was carrying the purple socks and he was worried because the mountainous path Father Quixote had taken was very rough for a man barefooted. Indeed, he came here and there on traces of blood. Several times he tried to shout Father Quixote's name, but the sound always died in his throat. Suddenly he emerged onto a great marble paving and there in front was the church of El Toboso from which strange sounds were coming. He went into the church, carrying the purple socks, and perched up on top of the altar like a sacred image was Father Quixote, and the congregation laughed and Father Quixote wept. The Mayor woke with the sense of a final, irreparable disaster. The dark had fallen. He was alone.

He went, as in his dream, to look for Father Quixote, and he was relieved to find him. Father Quixote had moved a little way down the slope, perhaps so as to be closer to Rocinante, perhaps because the ground was softer there. He had taken off his socks and made a pillow with them for his head with the help of his shoes and he was deeply asleep.

The Mayor hadn't the heart to wake him. The hour was too late to take the by-road to Osera now and the Mayor felt it much safer not to return to León. He again found his chosen spot out of sight of Father Quixote and he soon slept, untroubled by any dream.

When he woke the sun was up and he was no longer in the shade. It was time to be off, he thought, and to seek coffee in the next village. He needed coffee. Vodka never caused him any trouble, but too much wine upset him rather as a tiresome reformist would have done in the Party. He went to wake Father Quixote, but the priest was not in the place where he had left him, although the socks and the shoes which had served as a pillow were still there. He called Father Quixote's name several times without effect and the sound of his own voice recalled his dream. He sat down and waited, thinking that Father Quixote had probably gone to get rid of the wine in a private place. But he could hardly have taken ten minutes—no bladder could hold that quantity of liquid. Perhaps they were moving in circles and Father Quixote, after draining himself dry, had gone to find his friend's sleeping-place. So the Mayor returned there with the purple socks in his hand and this again brought back his dream in a disquieting way. Father Quixote was nowhere to be seen.

The Mayor thought: He may have gone to see whether Rocinante is safe. The day before, under the Mayor's instruction, Father Quixote had driven Rocinante a little way off the road behind a heap of sand left over from some long-ago road repairs, so that she would be almost invisible to any Guardia passing by.

Father Quixote was not beside the car, but Rocinante had company now—a Renault was parked behind her, and a young couple in blue jeans sat among the rocks with haversacks beside them which they were filling with cups and saucers and plates left over, judging by the debris, from a very good breakfast. The Mayor felt hungry at the sight. They seemed friendly, they greeted him with a smile, and

145

he asked with some hesitation, "I wonder if you could spare me a roll?"

They gazed at him, he thought, nervously. He realized how unshaven he was and that he was still carrying the purple socks. He could tell too that they were foreigners. The man said in an American accent, "I am afraid I don't understand much Spanish. *Parlez-vous français?*"

"*Un petit peu,*" the Mayor said, "*très petit peu.*"

"*Comme moi,*" the man said, and there was an awkward pause.

"*J'ai faim,*" the Mayor said. The quality of his French made him feel like a beggar. "*J'ai pensé si vous avez finis votre*"—he sought the word in vain—"*votre desayuno. . . .*"

"*Desayuno?*"

It was astonishing, the Mayor thought, how many foreign tourists went traveling around Spain without even knowing the most essential words.

"Ronald," the girl said in her incomprehensible tongue, "I'll go fetch the dictionary from the car."

The Mayor noticed when she got up that she had long attractive legs and he touched his cheek—a gesture of sadness for vanished youth. He said, "*Il faut me pardonner, Señorita. . . . Je n'ai pas . . .*" but he realized that he didn't know the French word for "shave." The two men stood facing each other in silence until she returned. Even then conversation was difficult. The Mayor said very slowly with a pause between each important word so that the girl had time to find it in her pocket dictionary, "If you have— finished—your breakfast—"

"*Desayuno* means breakfast," the girl told her companion with an air of delighted discovery.

"—could I have a *bollo?*"

"*Bollo*—a penny loaf, it says," the girl interpreted, "but ours cost a lot more than a penny."

"Dictionaries are always out of date," her companion said. "You can't expect them to keep up with inflation."

"I am very hungry," the Mayor told them, pronouncing the key word carefully.

The girl flicked her pages over. "*Ambriento*—wasn't that the word? I can't find it."

"Try with an 'h.' I don't think they pronounce the h's."

"Oh then, here it is. 'Eager.' But what's he eager for?"

"Isn't there another meaning?"

"Oh yes, how crazy of me. 'Hungry.' That must be it. He's hungry for a penny loaf."

"There are two left. Give him both. And look—give the poor devil this as well," and he handed her a hundred-peseta note.

The Mayor took the loaves and rejected the money. To explain the reason he pointed first at Rocinante and then at himself.

"My goodness," the girl said, "it's his car and we go and offer him a hundred pesetas." She put both hands together and raised them in a rather Eastern gesture. The Mayor smiled. He realized that it was an apology.

The young man said sullenly, "How was I to know?"

The Mayor began to eat one of the rolls. The girl searched in the dictionary. "*Mantequilla?*" she asked.

"Man take what?" her companion demanded in a disagreeable tone.

"I'm asking if he'd like some butter."

"I've finished it. It wasn't worth keeping."

The Mayor shook his head and finished the roll. He put the other one in his pocket. "*Para mi amigo*," he explained.

"Why! I understood that," the girl said with delight. "It's for his girl. Don't you remember in Latin—*amo* I love, *amas* you love? I've forgotten how it goes on. I bet they've been making out in the bush like us."

The Mayor put his hand to his mouth and shouted again, but there was no reply.

"How can you tell it's a girl?" the man asked. He was determined to be difficult. "In Spanish it's probably like in French. An *ami* can be any sex unless you see it written."

"Oh goodness," the girl said, "do you think it could be that corpse we saw them carrying . . . ?"

"We don't *know* it was a corpse. If it was a corpse why is he keeping that roll?"

"Ask him."

"How can I? You've got the dictionary."

The Mayor tried shouting again. Only a faint echo answered.

"It certainly looked like a corpse," the girl said.

"They may have been just taking him to hospital."

"You always have such *uninteresting* explanations of everything. Anyway, he wouldn't need a roll in hospital."

"In underdeveloped countries the relations often have to bring food to the patient."

"Spain isn't an underdeveloped country."

"That's what you say."

They seemed to be quarreling about something and the Mayor wandered back to Father Quixote's sleeping-place. The mystery of his disappearance and the memory of his dream weighed on the Mayor's spirits, and he returned to Rocinante.

In his absence they had consulted the dictionary with some effect. "*Camilla,*" the girl said, pronouncing it rather oddly so that the Mayor didn't at first catch the meaning.

"Are you sure that you've got it right?" the man asked. "It sounds more like a girl's name than a stretcher. I don't see why you looked up 'stretcher' anyway. They hadn't got a stretcher."

"But don't you see it conveys the meaning?" the girl insisted. "Can you find one word in the dictionary which would describe someone being carried past us by the head and the feet?"

148   "What about simply 'carried'?"

"The dictionary only gives the infinitive of verbs, but I'll try if you like. *Transportar*," she said, "*camilla*." The Mayor suddenly understood what she was trying to say, but it was all he did understand.

"*Dónde?*" he asked with a sense of despair, "*dónde?*"

"I think he means 'where,' " the man said, and he became suddenly an inspired communicator. He strode to his car, he opened the door, he bent double and appeared to shovel something heavy inside. Then he waved his arms in the direction of León and said, "Gone with the wind."

The Mayor sat abruptly down on a rock. What could have happened? Had the Guardia tracked them down? But surely the Guardia would have waited to catch Father Quixote's companion? And why should they carry Father Quixote off on a stretcher? Had they shot him and then taken fright at what they had done? His head was bowed under the pressure of his thoughts.

"Poor man," the girl whispered, "he's mourning for his dead friend. I think we'd better go away quietly."

They picked up their knapsacks and tiptoed to their car.

"It's sort of exciting," the girl said as she settled herself down, "but it's terribly, terribly sad, of course. I feel like I was in church."

PART TWO

1

MONSIGNOR QUIXOTE
ENCOUNTERS THE BISHOP

1

When Father Quixote opened his eyes he was surprised to see that the countryside was in rapid motion on
either side, while he lay quietly in almost the same position
as the one in which he had fallen asleep. Trees pelted past
him and then a house. He supposed his vision had been
affected by the wine which he had drunk, and with a sigh
at his lack of wisdom and a resolve to be more restrained in
future he closed them and was immediately asleep again.

He was half woken a second time by a strange jolting
motion that ceased abruptly and he felt his body sag and
come to rest on what seemed like a cold sheet instead of
the rather prickly ground on which he had been lying. It
was all very odd. He put his hand behind his head to adjust
the pillow which he had made out of his purple socks and
encountered a real pillow. A woman's voice said with indig-
nation, "And what in the name of the Blessed Virgin have
you done to the poor father?"

Another voice said, "Don't worry, woman. He'll wake up
in a minute. Go and make him a good strong cup of coffee."

"It's tea he always takes."

"Tea, then and make it strong. I'll stay here till he wakes

and so will. . . ." But Father Quixote slid again into the peace and the pleasure of sleep. He dreamt of three balloons which he had inflated and released into the air: two were big and one was small. This worried him. He wanted to catch the small one and blow it up to match the others. He woke again, blinked twice and realized quite clearly that he was home in El Toboso lying on his old bed. Fingers felt his pulse.

"Doctor Galván," he exclaimed. "You! What are you doing in El Toboso?"

"Don't worry," the doctor said soothingly. "You will soon be yourself again."

"Where is Sancho?"

"Sancho?"

"The Mayor."

"We left the fellow in his drunken sleep."

"Rocinante?"

"Your car? No doubt he'll bring it back. Unless, of course, he slips across the border."

"How did I come here?"

"I thought it best to give you a little injection. To calm you."

"Wasn't I calm?"

"You were asleep, but I thought that in the circumstances your reaction to our coming might make you— excitable."

"Who was the other?"

"What do you mean—the other?"

"You said 'our coming.' "

"Oh, your good friend Father Herrera was with me, of course."

"And you brought me here—against my will?"

"This is your home, my old friend—El Toboso. Where better could you stay and rest awhile?"

"I don't need any rest. You've even undressed me."

154   "We took off your outer things, that's all."

"My trousers!"

"You mustn't get excited. It's bad for you. Trust me— you need a short period of repose. The bishop himself appealed to Father Herrera to find you and bring you home before things went too far. Father Herrera telephoned to me in Ciudad Real. Teresa gave him my name and as I have a cousin in the Ministry of the Interior the Guardia were very understanding and helpful. It was so lucky that you telephoned to Teresa from León."

Teresa came into the room carrying a cup of tea. "Father, father," she said, "what a blessed thing it is to see you alive and well."

"Not quite well yet, Teresa," Doctor Galván corrected her, "but after a few weeks of quiet. . . ."

"Weeks of quiet indeed. I shall get up at once." He made an effort and sank down again on the bed.

"A bit giddy, eh? Don't worry. That merely comes from the injections. I had to give you two more on the road."

There was the gleam of a white collar catching the sun and Father Herrera stood in the doorway. "How is he?" he asked.

"Getting along nicely, nicely."

"You two have been guilty," Father Quixote said, "of a criminal action. Abduction, medical treatment without the patient's consent—"

"I had clear instructions from the bishop," Father Herrera replied, "to bring you home."

"*Que le den por el saco al obispo*," Father Quixote said, and a deathly silence followed his words. Even Father Quixote was shocked at himself. Where on earth could he have learned such a phrase, how was it that it came so quickly and unexpectedly to his tongue? From what remote memory? Then the silence was broken by a giggle. It was the first time Father Quixote had ever heard Teresa laugh. He said, "I must get up. At once. Where are my trousers?"

"I have them in my care," Father Herrera said. "The   155

words you have just used . . . I could never bring myself to repeat them . . . such words in the mouth of a priest, a monsignor. . . ."

Father Quixote felt a wild temptation to use the same unrepeatable phrase about his title of monsignor, but he resisted it. "Bring me my trousers at once," he said, "I want to get up."

"An obscene expression like that proves that you are not in your right mind."

"I told you to bring me my trousers."

"Patience, patience," Doctor Galván said. "In a few days. Now you need to rest. Above all, no excitement."

"My trousers!"

"They will remain in my care until you are better," Father Herrera said.

"Teresa!" Father Quixote appealed to his only friend.

"He's locked them up in a drawer. God forgive me, father. I didn't know what he intended."

"What do you expect me to do, lying here in bed?"

"A little meditation would not be amiss," Father Herrera said. "You have been behaving in a very curious way."

"What do you mean?"

"The Guardia at Avila reported that you had exchanged clothes with your companion and given a false address."

"A total misunderstanding."

"A bank robber arrested in León said that you gave him your shoes and hid him in your car."

"He wasn't a bank robber. It was only a self-service store."

"His Excellency and I had a lot of trouble persuading the Guardia to take no action. The bishop even had to telephone His Excellency at Avila to intercede. Doctor Galván's cousin was of great help also. And Doctor Galván too, of course. We were able at last to convince them that you were suffering from a nervous breakdown."

"That's nonsense."

"It's the most charitable explanation possible for your conduct. Anyway, we have narrowly avoided a great scandal in the Church." He qualified his statement. "So far at least."

"And now sleep a little," Doctor Galván told Father Quixote. "A little soup at midday," he instructed Teresa, "and perhaps an omelet in the evening. No wine for the moment. I'll drop in this evening and see how our patient is doing, but don't wake him up if he is asleep."

"And mind," Father Herrera told her, "to tidy up the sitting room while I am at Mass tomorrow morning. I don't know at what hour the bishop will be arriving."

"The bishop?" Teresa exclaimed and her question was echoed by Father Quixote.

Father Herrera did not bother to reply. He went out, closing the door not with a bang, but with what one might perhaps describe as a snap. Father Quixote turned his head on the pillow toward Doctor Galván. "Doctor," he said, "you are an old friend. You remember that time when I had pneumonia?"

"Of course I do. Let me think. It must have been nearly thirty years ago."

"Yes, I was very afraid to die in those days. I had so much on my conscience. I expect you've forgotten what you said to me."

"I suppose I told you to drink as much water as you could."

"No, it wasn't that." He searched in his memory, but the exact words wouldn't come. "You said something like this: think of the millions who are dying between one tick of the clock and the next—thugs and thieves and swindlers and schoolmasters and good fathers and mothers, bank managers and doctors, chemists and butchers—do you really believe He has the time to bother or to condemn?"

"Did I really say that?"

"More or less. You didn't know what a great comfort it was to me. Now you have heard Father Herrera—it's not God but the bishop who's coming to see me. I wish you had a word of comfort for *his* visit."

"That's altogether a more difficult problem," Doctor Galván said, "but perhaps you have already said it. 'Bugger the bishop.' "

2

Father Quixote strictly obeyed the advice of Doctor Galván. He slept as much as he could, he drank soup at midday, he ate half his omelet in the evening. He thought how much better cheese had tasted in the open air with a bottle of Manchegan wine.

He woke automatically at a quarter past five (for more than thirty years he had said Mass at six in the almost empty church). Now he lay in bed and listened for the sound of a door closing which would signal the departure of Father Herrera, but it was nearly seven before the clap came. Father Herrera had obviously altered the time of Mass. The pain this gave him he knew was quite unreasonable. Father Herrera in doing that might even add two or three to the congregation.

Father Quixote waited five minutes (for Father Herrera might possibly have forgotten something—a handkerchief perhaps) and then he stole on tiptoe to the living room. A sheet had been neatly folded on the armchair underneath a pillow. Father Herrera certainly had the virtue of tidiness if tidiness be a virtue. Father Quixote looked along his bookshelves. Alas! He had left his favorite reading in the care of Rocinante. Saint Francis de Sales, his usual comforter, was off somewhere on the roads of Spain. He picked out *The Confessions of Saint Augustine,* and the *Spiritual Letters* of the eighteenth-century Jesuit Father Caussade, which he had sometimes found consoling when he was a seminarian, and returned to bed. Teresa had heard his movements and brought him a cup of tea with a roll and butter. She was in a very bad mood.

"Who does he think I am?" she demanded. "Tidy up while he is at Mass. Haven't I tidied up for you for twenty years and more? I don't need him or the bishop to teach me my duty."

"You really think the bishop is coming?"

"Oh, they are thick as thieves, those two. On the telephone morning, noon and night ever since you left. Always Excellency, Excellency, Excellency. You would think he was talking to God himself."

"My ancestor," Father Quixote said, "was at least spared the bishop when the priest brought him home. And I prefer Doctor Galván to that stupid barber who told my ancestor all those tales about madmen. How could such stories of madmen have cured him if he had been really mad, which I don't for a moment believe. Oh well, we must look on the bright side, Teresa. I don't think they will try to burn my books."

"Not burn them perhaps, but Father Herrera told me how I was to keep your study locked. He said he didn't want you tiring your head with books. Anyway not till after the bishop had been."

"But you didn't lock the door, Teresa. You can see I have two books with me."

"Is it me who would lock you out of your own room, when it hurts me to see that young priest sit there as though it belonged to him? But better hide the books under the sheet when the bishop comes. They are two of a kind, those two."

He heard Father Herrera return from Mass; he heard the clatter of plates for the priest's breakfast—Teresa was making twice the noise in the kitchen as she would have made for him. He turned to Father Caussade, who was a more comforting presence to have at his bedside than Father Heribert Jone. He pretended to himself that Father Caussade was sitting beside his bed to hear his confession. Was it four days that had passed or five?

"Father, since my last confession ten days ago. . . ." He was worried again by the laughter which had so nearly come to him as he watched the film in Valladolid, and by the absence of any kind of desire which would prove him human and give him a sense of shame. Was it possible that he had even picked up in the cinema the vulgar phrase which he had used in talking of the bishop? But there had been no bishop in the film. The obscene words had caused Teresa to laugh and Doctor Galván had even repeated them. He said to Father Caussade, "If there was a sin in her laughter or in Doctor Galván's counsel, the sin was mine, mine only." There was a worse sin. Under the influence of wine he had minimized the importance of the Holy Ghost by comparing it to a half bottle of Manchegan. It was certainly a black record with which he had to face the reprobation of the bishop, but it was not really the bishop he feared. He feared himself. He felt as though he had been touched by the wing-tip of the worst sin of all, despair.

He opened Father Caussade's *Spiritual Letters* at random. The first passage he read had no relevance at all as far as he could understand it. "In my opinion your too frequent contact with your many relations and others in the world are a stumbling block to your advancement." Father Caussade, it was true, was writing to a nun, but all the same. . . . A priest and a nun are closely allied. I never wanted to be advanced, he protested to the empty air, I never wanted to be a monsignor, and I have no relatives except a second cousin in Mexico.

Without much hope he opened the book a second time, but this time he was rewarded, although the paragraph he had fixed on began discouragingly. "Have I ever in my life made a good confession? Has God pardoned me? Am I in a good or a bad state?" He was tempted to close the book but he read on. "I at once reply: God wishes to conceal all that from me, so that I may blindly abandon myself to His mercies. I do not wish to know what He does not wish to show me and I wish to proceed in the midst of whatever darkness He may plunge me into. It is His business to know the state of my progress, mine to occupy myself with Him alone. He will take care of all the rest; I leave it to Him."

" 'I leave it to Him,' " Father Quixote repeated aloud and at that moment the door of his room opened and Father Herrera's voice announced, "His Excellency is here."

Father Quixote had for a moment the odd impression that Father Herrera had suddenly grown old—the collar was the same blinding white, but the hair was white too and Father Herrera of course did not wear a bishop's ring or a big cross slung round his neck. But he would in time wear both, he certainly would in time, Father Quixote thought.

"I am sorry, Excellency. If you will give me a few minutes' grace I will be with you in the study."

"Stay where you are, monsignor," the bishop said. (He rolled out the title "monsignor" with an obvious bitterness.) He took from his sleeve a white silk handkerchief and dusted the chair beside the bed, looked carefully at the handkerchief to see how far it might have been soiled, lowered himself into the chair and put his hand on the sheet. But as Father Quixote was not in a position in which he could genuflect he thought it was permissible to leave out the kiss and the bishop after a brief pause withdrew his hand. Then the bishop pursed his lips and following a moment's reflection blew out the monosyllable: "Well!"

Father Herrera was standing in the doorway like a bodyguard. The bishop told him, "You can leave me and the monsignor"—the word seemed to burn his tongue for he made a grimace—"to have our little discussion alone." Father Herrera withdrew.

The bishop clutched the cross on his purple *pechera* as though he were seeking a higher than human wisdom. It seemed an anticlimax to Father Quixote when he said, "I trust you are feeling better."

"I am feeling perfectly well," Father Quixote replied. "My holiday has done me much good."

"Not if the reports I have received are true."

"What reports?"

"The Church always struggles to keep above politics."

"Always?"

"You know very well what I thought of your unfortunate involvement with the organization In Vinculis."

"It was an impromptu act of charity, Excellency. I admit that I didn't really think. Perhaps with charity one shouldn't think. Charity, like love, should be blind."

"You have been promoted for reasons quite beyond my comprehension to the rank of monsignor. A monsignor should always think. He must guard the dignity of the Church."

"I did not ask to be a monsignor. I do not like being a monsignor. The dignity of the parish priest of El Toboso is difficult enough to support."

"I do not pay attention to every rumor, monsignor. The mere fact that a man is a member of Opus Dei does not necessarily make him a reliable witness. I will take your word if you give it to me that you didn't go into a certain shop in Madrid and ask to buy a cardinal's hat."

"That was not me. My friend made a harmless little joke. . . ."

"Harmless? That friend of yours, I believe, is a former mayor of El Toboso. A Communist. You choose very unsuitable friends and traveling companions, monsignor."

"I don't need to remind Your Excellency that Our Lord—"

"Oh yes, yes. I know what you are going to say. The text about publicans and sinners has always been very carelessly used to justify a lot of imprudence. Saint Matthew, chosen by Our Lord, was a tax gatherer—a publican, a despised class. True enough, but there's a whole world of difference between a tax gatherer and a Communist."

"I suppose in some Eastern countries it's possible to be both."

"I would remind *you*, monsignor, that Our Lord was the Son of God. To Him all things were permissible, but for a poor priest like you and me isn't it more prudent to walk in the footsteps of Saint Paul? You know what he wrote to Titus—'There are many rebellious spirits abroad, who talk of their own fantasies and lead men's minds astray: they must be silenced.' "

The bishop paused to hear Father Quixote's response but none came. Perhaps he took this for a good sign, for when he spoke next, he dropped the "monsignor" and used the friendly and companionable "father." "Your friend, father," he said, "had apparently been drinking very heavily when you were both found. He didn't even wake when they spoke to him. Father Herrera noticed too that there was a great deal of wine in your car. I realize that in your nervous condition wine must have proved a serious temptation. Personally I always leave wine to the Mass. I prefer water. I like to pretend when I take a glass that I am drinking the pure water of Jordan."

"Perhaps not so pure," Father Quixote said.

"What do you mean, father?"

"Well, Excellency, I can't help thinking of how Naaman, the Syrian, bathed seven times in the Jordan and left all his leprosy behind him in the water."

"An old Jewish legend from a very long time ago."

"Yes, I know that, Excellency, but still—after all it may be a true history—and leprosy is a mysterious disease. How many good Jewish lepers may have followed the example of Naaman? Of course I agree with you that Saint Paul is a reliable guide and you will certainly remember that he also wrote to Titus—no, I am wrong, it was to Timothy: 'Do not confine thyself to water any longer: take a little wine to relieve thy stomach.' "

A period of silence descended on the bedroom. Father Quixote thought that perhaps the bishop was seeking another quotation from Saint Paul, but he was wrong. The pause represented a change of subject rather than of mood. "What I don't understand, monsignor, is that the Guardia found that you had exchanged clothes with this—this ex-Mayor, this Communist."

"There was not an exchange of clothes, Excellency, only of a collar."

The bishop closed his eyes. Impatience? Or he might have been praying for understanding.

"Why even a collar?"

"He thought I must be suffering from the heat in that kind of collar, so I gave it to him to try. I didn't want him to think I was claiming any special merit. . . . A military uniform or even a Guardia's must be more difficult to endure in the heat than a collar. We are the lucky ones, Excellency."

"A story came to the ears of the parish priest in Valladolid that a bishop—or a monsignor—had been seen coming out of a scandalous film there—you know the kind of films which are shown now since the Generalissimo died. . . ."

"Perhaps the poor monsignor did not know the kind of film he was attending. Sometimes titles are misleading."

"What was so shocking in the story is that the bishop—or the monsignor—you know how people can be confused by the *pechera* which you and I both wear—was seen coming out of this disreputable cinema laughing."

"Not laughing, Excellency. Perhaps smiling."

"I don't understand your presence at such a film."

"I was deceived by the innocence of the title."

"Which was?"

"*A Maiden's Prayer.*"

The bishop gave a deep sigh. "I sometimes wish," he said, "that the title of maiden were confined to Our Lady—and perhaps to members of religious orders. I realize you have been leading a very retired life in El Toboso, and you do not realize that the word 'maiden' used in our great cities in its purely temporary sense is often an incitement to lust."

"I admit, Excellency, that it had not occurred to me."

"Of course these are very minor matters in the eyes of the Guardia Civil, however scandalous they may appear in the eyes of the Church. But I and my colleague at Avila have had very great difficulty in persuading them to shut their eyes for what was a grave *criminal* offense. We had to approach a high authority in the Ministry of the Interior—luckily a member of Opus Dei. . . ."

"And a cousin, I believe, of Doctor Galván?"

"That is hardly relevant. He saw at once that it would do the Church untold harm if a monsignor appeared in the dock charged with helping a murderer to escape—"

"Not a murderer, Excellency. He missed."

"A bank robber."

"No, no. It was a self-service store."

"I wish you wouldn't interrupt me with petty details. The

165

Guardia in León found the man in possession of your shoes clearly marked inside with your name."

"It's a stupid habit of Teresa's. Poor thing, she means well, but she never trusts the cobbler to give the right pair back when he resoles them."

"I don't know whether it's deliberate, monsignor, but you always seem to bring into our serious discussion quite trivial and irrelevant details."

"I am sorry—it wasn't my intention—I thought it might seem odd to you, my shoes being marked that way."

"What seems odd to me is your helping this criminal to escape the law."

"He did have a gun—but of course he would not have used it. Shooting us would hardly have helped him."

"The Guardia in the end accepted that explanation, although the man had got rid of the gun and denied ever having had one. All the same they seem to have established that first you had hidden the man in the boot of your car and lied to a Guardia. You can't have done that under threat."

"I didn't lie, Excellency. Perhaps—well, I indulged in a little equivocation. The Guardia never directly asked whether he was in the boot. Of course I could plead a 'broad mental restriction.' Father Heribert Jone points out that an accused criminal—I was, legalistically speaking, a criminal—may plead 'not guilty' which is only a conventional way of saying, 'I am not guilty before law until I am proved guilty.' He even allows the criminal to say that the accusation is a calumny and may offer proofs for his pretended innocence—but there I think Father Heribert Jone goes a little too far."

"Who on earth is Father Heribert Jone?"

"A distinguished German moral theologian."

"I thank God that he's not a Spaniard."

"Father Herrera has a great respect for him."

"Anyway, I haven't come here to talk about moral theology."

"I have always found it a very confusing subject, Excellency. For instance I can't help wondering now about the concept of Natural Law. . . ."

"Nor have I come to talk about Natural Law. You have a remarkable talent, monsignor, for straying from the real subject."

"Which is, Excellency?"

"The scandals you have been causing."

"But if I am accused of lies . . . surely we are somewhere in the realm of moral theology."

"I am trying very, very hard to believe"—and the bishop gave another prolonged sigh which made Father Quixote wonder with pity, and not with satisfaction, whether the bishop might possibly be suffering from asthma—"I repeat *very* hard, that you are too ill to realize what a dangerous situation you are in."

"Well, I suppose that applies to all of us."

"To all of us?"

"When we begin to think, I mean."

The bishop gave a curious sound—it reminded Father Quixote of one of Teresa's hens laying an egg. "Ah," the bishop said, "I was coming to that. Dangerous thought. Your Communist companion no doubt led you to think in ways—"

"It wasn't that he *led* me, Excellency. He gave me the opportunity. You know in El Toboso—I'm very fond of the garagist (he looks after Rocinante so well), the butcher is a bit of a scoundrel—I don't mean that there's anything profoundly wrong in scoundrels, and of course there are the nuns who do make excellent cakes, but on this holiday I have felt a freedom. . . ."

"A very dangerous freedom it seems to have been."

"But He gave it to us, didn't He—freedom? That was why they crucified Him."

"Freedom," the bishop said. It was like an explosion. "Freedom to break the law? You, a monsignor? Freedom to go to pornographic films? Help murderers?"

"No, no, I told you that he missed."

"And your companion—a Communist. Talking politics. . . ."

"No, no. We've discussed much more serious things than politics. Though I admit I hadn't realized that Marx had so nobly defended the Church."

"Marx?"

"A much misunderstood man, Excellency. I promise you."

"What books have you been reading on this—extraordinary—expedition?"

"I always take with me Saint Francis de Sales. To please Father Herrera I took Father Heribert Jone with me too. And my friend lent me *The Communist Manifesto*—no, no, Excellency, it's not at all what you think it is. Of course I cannot agree with all his ideas, but there is a most moving tribute to religion—he speaks of 'The most heavenly ecstasies of religious fervor.' "

"I cannot sit here any longer and listen to the ravings of a sick mind," the bishop said and rose.

"I have kept you here far too long, Excellency. It was a great act of charity on your part to come to see me in El Toboso. Doctor Galván will assure you that I am quite well."

"In the body perhaps. I think you need a different kind of doctor. I shall consult Doctor Galván, of course, before I write to the archbishop. And I shall pray."

"I am very grateful for your prayers," Father Quixote said. He noticed that the bishop did not offer him his ring before leaving. Father Quixote reproached himself for having spoken too freely. I have upset the poor man, he thought. Bishops, just like the very poor and the uneducated, should be treated with a special prudence.

Whispers were to be heard from the passage outside his door. Then a key turned in the lock. So I am a prisoner, he thought, like Cervantes.

II

MONSIGNOR QUIXOTE'S
SECOND JOURNEY

1

It was the toot-toot-toot of a car which woke Father Quixote. Even in his sleep he had recognized the unmistakable tone of Rocinante—a plaintive tone, without the anger, the petulance or the impatience of a big car—a tone which simply said encouragingly, "I am here if you want me." He went at once to the window and looked out, but Rocinante must have been parked somewhere out of his view, for the only car in sight was colored a bright blue and not a rusty red. He went to the door, quite forgetting that it was locked, and shook the handle. Teresa's voice answered him, "Hush, father. Give him another minute."

"Give who another minute?"

"Father Herrera's gone off to confession, but he never stays long in the box if there's no one waiting, so I've told the young fellow at the garage he has to go quickly up to the church before Father Herrera leaves and keep him busy with a long confession."

Father Quixote felt completely at sea. This was not the life he had known for so many decades in El Toboso. What had brought about the change?

"Can you unlock the door, Teresa? Rocinante has returned."

"Yes. I know. I would never have recognized her, poor dear, with all that bright blue paint she has on and a new number even."

"Please, Teresa, unlock the door. I must see what has happened to Rocinante."

"I can't, father, for I haven't the key, but don't worry, he'll manage all right if you give him another minute."

"Who?"

"The Mayor, of course."

"The Mayor. Where is he?"

"He's in your study, where else would he be? Breaking open your cupboard which Father Herrera locked—with one of my hairpins and a bottle of olive oil."

"Why olive oil?"

"I wouldn't know, father, but I trust him."

"What's in the cupboard?"

"Your trousers, father, and all your upper clothes."

"If he can open the cupboard can't he open this door?"

"It's what I said to him, but he spoke of what he calls priorities."

Father Quixote tried to wait with a patience hardly encouraged by a running commentary from Teresa. "Oh, I thought he got it open, but it's still stuck fast and now he's got one of Father Herrera's razor blades. There'll be hell to pay because Father Herrera keeps a regular count of them. . . . Now he's broken the blade and God's sakes he's at work with Father Herrera's nail scissors. . . . Wait a bit—be patient—God be thanked, it's coming open. Only I hope he does your door quicker or we'll be having Father Herrera back—the young boy at the garage hasn't all that imagination."

"Are you all right, father?" came the Mayor's voice from the other side of the door.

"I'm all right, but what have you been doing to Rocinante?"

171

"I stopped off with my friend at Valladolid and fixed her so that the Guardia won't recognize her—not at first sight, anyway. Now I'm going to work on your door."

"You don't have to. I can get through the window."

It was lucky, he thought, that there was no one there to see the parish priest climbing through the window in pajamas and knocking on his own front door. Teresa retired discreetly to the kitchen and Father Quixote dressed hurriedly in his study. "You've certainly made a mess of that cupboard door," he said.

"It was more difficult to open than I thought. What are you looking for?"

"My collar."

"Here's one. And I've got your bib in the car."

"It has caused me a lot of trouble already. I'm not going to wear it, Sancho."

"But we'll take it with us. It may prove useful. One never knows."

"I can't find any socks."

"I have your purple socks. And your new shoes too."

"It was the old ones I was looking for. I'm sorry. Of course they've gone forever."

"They are in the hands of the Guardia."

"Yes. I forgot. The bishop told me. I suppose we must go. I hope the poor bishop won't have a stroke."

A letter caught his eye. It should have caught his eye before because it was propped up against one of his old seminary volumes and enthroned on two others. The writer had obviously intended it to be conspicuous. He looked at the envelope and put it into his pocket.

"What's that?" the Mayor asked.

"A letter from the bishop, I think. I know his writing too well."

"Aren't you going to read it?"

"Bad trouble can wait until we've had a bottle of Manchegan."

He went into the kitchen to say goodbye to Teresa. "I really don't know how you are going to explain matters to Father Herrera."

"It's he who will have to do all the explaining. What reason had he got to lock you up in your very own room in your own house and take your own clothes?"

He kissed Teresa on her forehead, something which he had never ventured to do before in all the years they had been together. "God bless you, Teresa," he said. "You have been very good to me. And patient. For a very long time."

"Tell me where you are going, father."

"It's better you shouldn't know because they'll all be asking you that. But I can tell you I'm going, God willing, to take a long rest in a quiet place."

"With that Communist?"

"Don't talk like the bishop, Teresa. The Mayor has been a good friend to me."

"I don't see the likes of him taking a long rest in a quiet place."

"You never know, Teresa. Stranger things have happened on the road already."

He turned, but her voice called him back. "Father, I feel as though we are saying goodbye forever."

"No, no, Teresa, for a Christian there's no such thing as goodbye forever."

He raised his hand from habit to make the sign of the cross in blessing, but he didn't complete it.

"I believe what I told her," he told himself as he went to find the Mayor, "I believe it of course, but how is it that when I speak of belief, I become aware always of a shadow, the shadow of disbelief haunting my belief?"

•

2

"Where do we go from here?" the Mayor asked.

"Do we have to make plans, Sancho? Last time we went a bit here and a bit there, at random. You won't agree, of course, but in a way we left ourselves in the hands of God."

"Then he wasn't a very reliable guide. You were brought back here, a prisoner, to El Toboso."

"Yes. Who knows? God moves very mysteriously—perhaps He wanted me to meet the bishop."

"For the bishop's sake—or yours?"

"How can I tell? At least I learned something from the bishop, though I doubt if he learned anything from me. But who can be sure?"

"So where does your God propose we go now?"

"Why don't we just follow our old route?"

"The Guardia might have the same idea. When the bishop warns them that we are loose again."

"Not exactly the same route. I don't want to go back to Madrid—nor Valladolid. They haven't left very happy memories—except the house of the historian."

"Historian?"

"The great Cervantes."

"We have to decide quickly, father. South is too hot. So do we go north towards the Basques or to the Galicians?"

"I agree."

"Agree to what? You didn't answer my question."

"Let's leave the details to God."

"And who drives? Are you sure that God has passed His driving test?"

"Of course I must drive. Rocinante would never understand if I sat in the car as a passenger."

"At least let us go at a reasonable speed. My friend at Valladolid said she was quite capable of eighty kilometers or even a hundred."

"He can't judge Rocinante from a brief inspection."

"I won't argue now. It's time to be off."

But they were not able to leave El Toboso so easily. Father Quixote had only just ground his way into low gear when a voice called, "Father, father." A boy was running up the road behind them.

"Don't pay any attention," the Mayor said. "We've got to get out of here."

"I must stop. It's the boy who works the pumps at the garage."

He was quite out of breath when he reached them.

"Well, what is it?" Father Quixote asked.

"Father," he said between pants, "father."

"I said, what is it?"

"I've been refused absolution, father. Shall I go to Hell?"

"I very much doubt it. What have you done? Have you murdered Father Herrera? I don't mean that would necessarily entail going to Hell. If you had a good enough reason."

"How could I have murdered him when it's him that's refused me?"

"Logically put. Why did he refuse you?"

"He said I was making a mock of the confessional."

"Oh dear, I was forgetting. It was you that Teresa sent. . . . It was very wrong of her. All the same she meant it in a good cause and I'm sure you'll both be forgiven. But she did tell me that you had no imagination. Why did Father Herrera refuse you absolution? What on earth did you go and invent?"

"I only told him I'd slept with a lot of girls."

"There aren't all that many in El Toboso except for the nuns. You didn't tell him you slept with a nun, did you?"

"I would never say such a thing, father. I'm secretary of the Children of Mary."

175

"And Father Herrera will surely end up in Opus Dei," the Mayor said. "For God's sake, let's be gone."

"What exactly did you say and he say?"

"I said, 'Bless me, father. I have sinned—' "

"No, no, leave out all those preliminaries."

"Well, I told him I'd been late at Mass and he asked me how many times and I said twenty and then I told him I'd lied a bit and he asked how many times and I said forty-five."

"You did go in for rather big figures, didn't you? And then?"

"Well, I couldn't think of anything more to say and I was afraid Teresa would be angry if I couldn't keep him any longer."

"You tell her from me when you see her that she'd better be on her knees tomorrow at confession."

"And then he asked me if I had sinned against purity and that gave me an idea, so I said, well, I had slept with some girls, and he asked me how many girls and I said around sixty-five, and it was then he got angry and he turned me out of the box."

"I don't wonder."

"Is it Hell I'll be going to?"

"If anyone is going to Hell it will be Teresa and you can tell her I said so."

"It's an awful lot of lies I told in the confessional. I was only late for Mass the once and I had good reason—there were so many tourists at the pumps."

"And the lies?"

"Two or three at most."

"And the girls?"

"You won't find one of them who'll do anything serious in El Toboso for fear of the nuns."

The Mayor said, "I can see Father Herrera coming down
176   the street from the church."

"Listen to me," Father Quixote said. "Make an act of contrition and promise me you won't lie any more in the confessional, not even if Teresa asks you to."

He was silent while the boy mumbled something. "And your promise?"

"Oh, I promise, father. Why shouldn't I? I don't go to confession anyway more than once a year."

"Say 'I promise before you, father, to God.' "

The boy repeated the words and Father Quixote gave him absolution, speaking rapidly.

The Mayor said, "That damned priest is only about a hundred paces away, father, and he's putting on speed."

Father Quixote started the engine and Rocinante responded with the jump of an antelope.

"Only just in time," the Mayor said. "But he's running nearly as fast as Rocinante. Oh, thank God, that boy's a treasure. He's put out his foot and tripped him up."

"If there was anything wrong about that confession, the fault was mine," Father Quixote said. Whether he was addressing himself, God or the Mayor will always remain uncertain.

"At least push Rocinante up to fifty. The old girl's not even trying. That priest will be on to the Guardia in no time."

"There's not so much hurry as you think," Father Quixote said. "He'll have an awful lot to say to that boy and after that he'll want to speak to the bishop and the bishop won't be home for quite a while."

"He might speak to the Guardia first."

"Not on your life. He has the prudent soul of a secretary."

They reached the high road to Alicante and the Mayor broke silence. "Left," he said sharply.

"Not to Madrid, surely? Anywhere but to Madrid."

"No cities," the Mayor said. "Wherever there's a country 177 road we'll take it. I'll feel safer when we reach the mountains. I suppose you haven't a passport?"

"No."

"Then Portugal is no refuge."

"Refuge from what? From the bishop?"

"You don't seem to realize, father, what a grave crime you have committed. You've freed a galley-slave."

"Poor fellow. All he got was my shoes and they were not much better than his own. He was doomed to failure. I always feel that those who always fail—he even ran out of petrol—are nearer to God than we are. Of course I shall pray to my ancestor for him. How often the Don knew failure. Even with the windmills."

"Then you'd better pray hard to him for both of us."

"Oh, I do. I do. We haven't failed enough yet, Sancho. Here we are again, you and I and Rocinante on the road, and at liberty."

It took them more than two hours to reach a small town called Mora, traveling by a roundabout route. There they found themselves on the main road to Toledo, but only for a matter of minutes. "We have to get into the mountains of Toledo," the Mayor said. "This road is not for us." They turned and twisted and for a while, on a very rough track, they seemed, judging from the sun, to be making a half circle.

"Do you know where we are?" Father Quixote asked.

"More or less," the Mayor replied unconvincingly.

"I can't help feeling a little hungry, Sancho."

"Your Teresa has given us enough sausage and cheese for a week."

"A week?"

"No hotels for us. No main roads."

They found a spot high in the mountains of Toledo, a comfortable place for eating, where they could drive off the road and conceal themselves and Rocinante. There was a stream too to chill their bottles as it trickled down to a lake below them which with difficulty the Mayor identified on the map as the Torre de Abraham—"Though why they named it after that old scoundrel I wouldn't know."

"Why do you call him a scoundrel?"

"Wasn't he prepared to kill his son? Oh, of course, there was a much worse scoundrel—the one you call God—he actually performed the ugly deed. What an example *he* set, and Stalin killed his spiritual sons in imitation. He very nearly killed Communism along with them just as the Curia has killed the Catholic Church."

"Not entirely, Sancho. Here beside you is at least one Catholic in spite of the Curia."

"Yes, and here is one Communist who is still alive in spite of the Politburo. We are survivors, you and I, father. Let us drink to that," and he fetched a bottle from the stream.

"To two survivors," Father Quixote said and raised his glass. He had a very healthy thirst, and it always surprised him to think how seldom his ancestor's biographer had spoken of wine. One could hardly count the adventure of the wineskins which the Don had broached in mistake for his enemies. He refilled his glass. "It seems to me," he told the Mayor, "that you have more belief in Communism than in the Party."

"And I was just going to say almost the same, father, that you seem to have more belief in Catholicism than in Rome."

"Belief? Oh, belief. Perhaps you are right, Sancho. But perhaps it's not belief that really matters."

"What do you mean, father? I thought. . . ."

"Did the Don really believe in Amadis of Gaul, Roland and all his heroes—or was it only that he believed in the virtues they stood for?"

"We are getting into dangerous waters, father."

"I know, I know. In your company, Sancho, I think more freely than when I am alone. When I am alone I read—I hide myself in my books. In them I can find the faith of better men than myself, and when I find that my belief is growing weak with age, like my body, then I tell myself that I must be wrong. My faith tells me I must be wrong—or is it only the faith of those better men? Is it my own faith that speaks to me or the faith of Saint Francis de Sales? And does it so much matter anyway? Give me some cheese. How wine makes me talk."

"Do you know what drew me to you in El Toboso, father? It wasn't that you were the only educated man in the place. I'm not so fond of the educated as all that. Don't talk to me of the intelligentsia or culture. You drew me to you because I thought you were the opposite of myself. A man gets tired of himself, of that face he sees every day when he shaves, and all my friends were in just the same mold as myself. I would go to Party meetings in Ciudad Real when it became safe after Franco was gone, and we called ourselves 'comrade' and we were a little afraid of each other because we knew each other as well as each one knew himself. We quoted Marx and Lenin to one another like passwords to prove we could be trusted, and we never spoke of the doubts which came to us on sleepless nights. I was drawn to you because I thought you were a man without doubts. I was drawn to you, I suppose, in a way by envy."

"How wrong you were, Sancho. I am riddled by doubts. I am sure of nothing, not even of the existence of God, but doubt is not treachery as you Communists seem to think. Doubt is human. Oh, I want to believe that it is all true—and that want is the only certain thing I feel. I want others to believe too—perhaps some of their belief might rub off on me. I think the baker believes."

"That was the belief I thought you had."

180   "Oh no, Sancho, then perhaps I could have burnt my

books and lived really alone, knowing that all was true. 'Knowing'? How terrible that might have been. Oh well, was it your ancestor or mine who used to say, 'Patience and shuffle the cards'?"

"Some sausage, father?"

"I think today I'll stick to cheese. Sausage is for stronger men."

"Perhaps today I'll stick to cheese too."

"Shall we open another bottle?"

"Why not?"

It was over the second bottle as the afternoon advanced that Sancho said, "I have something to confess to you, father. Oh, not in the confessional. I'm not asking any forgiveness from that myth of yours or mine up there, only from you." He brooded over his glass. "If I hadn't come to fetch you, what would have happened?"

"I don't know. I think the bishop believes I am mad. Perhaps they would have tried to put me in an asylum, though I don't think Doctor Galván would have agreed to help them. What is the legal position for a man with no relations? Can he be put away against his will? Perhaps the bishop, with Father Herrera to help him. . . . And then in the background, of course, there is always the archbishop. . . . They will never forget that time when I gave a little money to In Vinculis."

"My friendship for you began then, though we'd hardly spoken."

"It's like learning to say the Mass. In the seminary one learns never to forget. Oh my goodness, I had quite forgotten. . . ."

"What?"

"The bishop left a letter for me." Father Quixote drew it from his pocket and turned it over and over.

"Go on, man. Open it. It's not a death warrant."

"How do you know?"

"The days of Torquemada are over."

"As long as there is a Church there will always be little Torquemadas. Give me another glass of wine." He drank it slowly to delay the moment of truth.

Sancho took the letter from him and opened it. He said, "It's short enough anyway. What does *Suspensión a Divinis* mean?"

"As I thought, it's the sentence of death," Father Quixote said. "Give me the letter." He put his glass down unfinished. "I'm not afraid any longer. After death there's nothing more they can do. There remains only the mercy of God." He read the letter aloud.

" 'My dear Monsignor, It was a great grief to me to hear you confirm the truth of the accusations which I had felt almost sure must have been due to misunderstanding, exaggeration or malice.' What a hypocrite! Oh well, I suppose hypocrisy in a bishop is almost necessary and would be considered by Father Heribert Jone a very venial sin. 'All the same, under the circumstances I am ready to think that your exchange of clothes with your Communist companion was not a symbolic act of defiance towards the Holy Father but was due to some severe mental disturbance, which also induced you to help a felon to escape and to visit without shame in your purple *pechera* as a monsignor a disgusting and pornographic film clearly denoted with an "S" to mark its true character. I have discussed your case with Doctor Galván who agrees with me that a long rest is indicated and I shall be writing to the Archbishop. In the meanwhile I find it my duty to announce to you a *Suspensión a Divinis.*' "

"What does that sentence of death mean exactly?"

"It means I mustn't say the Mass—not in public, not even in private. But in the privacy of my room I shall say it, for I am innocent. I must hear no confessions either— except in an extreme emergency. I remain a priest, but a priest only to myself. A useless priest forbidden to serve others. I'm glad you came to fetch me. How could I have borne that sort of life in El Toboso?"

"You could appeal to Rome. You are a monsignor."

"Even a monsignor can be lost in those dusty Curia files."

"I told you I had something to confess, father. I nearly didn't come." It was the Mayor now who drank to give himself the courage to speak. "When I found you gone—there were two Americans nearby who saw what happened, they thought you were dead but I knew better—I thought, 'I'll borrow Rocinante and make for Portugal.' I have good friends in the Party there and I thought I would stay awhile until all the fuss was over."

"But you didn't go."

"I drove to Ponferrada and there I took the main road to Orense. On my map there was a side road which I meant to take, for it was less than sixty kilometers from there to the frontier." He shrugged his shoulders. "Oh well, I got to the side road and I turned and I drove back to Valladolid and I asked my comrade in the garage to paint the car and change the number again."

"But why didn't you go on?"

"I looked at your damn purple socks and your bib, and your new shoes which we had bought in León, and I remembered suddenly the way you had blown up that balloon."

"They seem insufficient reasons."

"They were sufficient for me."

"I'm glad you came, Sancho. I feel safe here with you and with Rocinante, safer than back there with Father Herrera. El Toboso is no longer home to me and I have no other, except here on this spot of ground with you."

"We've got to find you another home, father, but where?"

"Somewhere quiet where Rocinante and I can rest for a while."

"And where the Guardia and the bishop won't find you."

"There was that Trappist monastery you spoke of in Galicia. . . . But *you* wouldn't feel at home there, Sancho."

"I could leave you with them and hire a car in Orense to take me across the border."

"I don't want our travels to end. Not before death, Sancho. My ancestor died in his bed. Perhaps he would have lived longer if he had stayed on the road. I'm not ready for death yet, Sancho."

"I'm worrying about the Guardia's computers. Rocinante is pretty well disguised, but at the frontier they may be looking out for the two of us."

"Like it or not, Sancho, I think you will have to stay for a week or two with the Trappists."

"The food will be bad."

"And the wine too perhaps."

"We had better stock up with some Galician wine on the road. The Manchegan is nearly finished."

III
HOW MONSIGNOR QUIXOTE
HAD HIS
LAST ADVENTURE
AMONG THE MEXICANS

1

They slept out for three nights, making their way with caution by little-frequented roads, from the mountains of Toledo, over the Sierra de Guadalupe, where Rocinante found it a strain when she climbed to over eight hundred meters, only to find it a yet greater strain when they reached the Sierra de Gredos where the road wound up to over fifteen hundred meters, for they avoided Salamanca and headed for the Duero river which separated them from the safety of Portugal. It was a very slow progress which they made through the mountains, but the Mayor preferred the mountains to the plains of Castile because of the long perspectives where an official jeep could be seen from far away and the villages were too small to contain a Guardia post. A sinuous progress it was on third-class roads, for they avoided even the dangerous second-class yellow ones on the map. As for the great red roads, these they banned completely.

It was always cold when the dark fell, and they were glad to substitute whiskey for wine to drink with the cheese and sausage. They slept afterwards with difficulty curled up in the car. When at last they were forced to come down into the plain the Mayor looked with longing at a signpost which pointed to Portugal. "If you only had a passport," he said, "we would make for Bragança. I prefer my comrades there to the Spanish ones. Cunhal is a better man than Carrillo."

"I thought Carrillo was a good man as Communists go."

"You can't trust a Euro-Communist."

"Surely you are not a Stalinist, Sancho?"

"I'm not a Stalinist, but at least you know where you are with them. They are not Jesuits. They don't turn with the wind. If they are cruel, they are cruel also to themselves. When you come to the end of the longest road of all you have to lie down and take a rest—a rest from arguments and theories and fashions. You can say, 'I don't believe but I accept,' and you fall into silence like the Trappists do. The Trappists are the Stalinists of the Church."

"Then you would have made a good Trappist, Sancho."

"Perhaps, though I don't like getting up early in the morning."

After they had crossed into Galicia they halted at a village so that the Mayor could enquire where there was a vineyard at which they could buy good wine, for they were down to the last bottle of Manchegan, and the Mayor distrusted all wine with labels. He was away for a full ten minutes and he had a somber air when he returned, so that Father Quixote asked with anxiety, "Bad news?"

"Oh, I have an address," he said and he described the route they must follow, and for the next half hour he said nothing, indicating the turnings to take with his hand, but his silence was so heavily loaded that Father Quixote insisted on piercing through it. "You are worried," he said. "Is it about the Guardia?"

"Oh, the Guardia," the Mayor exclaimed. "We can deal with the Guardia. Haven't we dealt with them well enough near Avila and on the road to León? I spit on the Guardia."

"Then what's upsetting you?"

"I don't like anything that I cannot understand."

"And what's that?"

"These ignorant villagers and their atrocious accents."

"They are Galicians, Sancho."

"And they know that we are foreigners. They think we will believe anything."

"What have they told you?"

"They pretended to be very solicitous about the wine. They argued among themselves about three vineyards—the white was better in one, the red in another, and their last words were a warning—they pretended to be very earnest about it. They took me for a fool because I was a foreigner. The insularity of these Galicians! You will find the best wine in Spain, they told me as though our Manchegan was just horses' piss."

"But what was the warning?"

"One of the vineyards was near a place called Learig. They said, 'Keep away from that one. The Mexicans are everywhere.' Those were their last words to me. They shouted them after me. 'Stay away from the land of the Mexicans. Their priests spoil even the wine.' "

"Mexicans! Are you sure you heard right?"

"I'm not deaf."

"What could they possibly mean?"

"I suppose Pancho Villa has risen from the dead and is sacking Galicia."

Another half an hour and they had entered a land of wine. On their right hand the southern slopes were green with vines, and on their left a decrepit village lay, like an abandoned corpse, along a cliffside, a house here and there in ruins, a mouth of broken teeth.

The Mayor said, "We don't take the road to the village. We go fifty yards on and leave the car and take a path up."

"Up to where?"

"They called him Señor Diego. In the end those fools   187

agreed that his was the best wine. 'The Mexicans haven't got there yet,' they said."

"The Mexicans again. I begin to be a little nervous, Sancho."

"Courage, father. You were not daunted by the windmills, why be daunted by a few Mexicans? That must be the path, so we leave the car here." They parked Rocinante behind a Mercedes which had already usurped the best place.

As they began to climb the path a stout man who wore a smart suit and a startling striped tie came hurrying down it. He was muttering angry words to himself. They narrowly avoided a collision when he stopped abruptly and blocked their way. "Are you going up there to buy wine?" he snapped at them.

"Yes."

"Give it up," the man said. "He's mad."

"Who's mad?" the Mayor asked.

"Señor Diego, of course. Who else? He's got a cellar full of good wine up there and he won't let me try a single glass, though I was ready to take a dozen cases. He said he didn't like my tie."

"There could be a difference of opinion about your tie," the Mayor said with caution.

"I'm a businessman myself, and I tell you it's not the way to do business. But now it's too late to get the wine elsewhere."

"Why all the hurry?"

"Because I promised the priest. I always keep a promise. It's good business to keep a promise. I promised the priest to get the wine. It's a promise to the Church."

"What does the Church want with a dozen cases of wine?"

"It's not only my promise. I may lose my place in the
procession. Unless the priest will accept cash instead. He

won't take checks. Get out of my way, please. I can't stay here talking, but I wanted to warn you. . . ."

"I don't understand what's going on," Father Quixote said.

"Nor do I."

At the head of the path there was a house much in need of repair and a table under a fig tree on which lay the remains of a meal. A young man in blue jeans came hurriedly towards them. He said, "Señor Diego will see nobody today."

"We have only come to buy a little wine," the Mayor said.

"I'm afraid that's not possible. Not today. And there's no use telling me about the feast. Señor Diego will have nothing to do with the feast."

"We don't want it for any feast. We are simple travelers and we've run out of wine."

"You are not Mexicans?"

"No, we are not Mexicans," Father Quixote said with a note of conviction. "Of your charity, father. . . . Just a few bottles of wine. We are on our way to the Trappists at Osera."

"The Trappists . . . ? How do you know I am a priest?"

"When you have been a priest as long as I have you will recognize a colleague. Even without his collar."

"This is Monsignor Quixote of El Toboso," the Mayor said.

"A monsignor?"

"Forget the 'monsignor,' father. A parish priest, as I suspect you are."

The young man ran towards the house. He called, "Señor Diego, Señor Diego. Come quickly. A monsignor. We have a monsignor here."

"Is it so rare to see a monsignor in this place?" the Mayor asked.

189

"Rare? It certainly is. The priests round here—they are all friends of the Mexicans."

"That man we met on the path—was he a Mexican?"

"Of course he was. One of the bad Mexicans. That's why Señor Diego wouldn't sell him any wine."

"I thought perhaps it was because of his tie."

An old man with great dignity came out onto the terrace. He had the sad and weary face of a man who has seen too much of life for far too long. He hesitated a moment between the Mayor and Father Quixote before, holding out both hands toward the Mayor, he made the wrong choice. "Welcome, monsignor, to my house."

"No, no," the young priest exclaimed, "the other one."

Señor Diego turned his hands first and then his eyes towards Father Quixote. "Forgive me," he said, "my sight is not what it was. I see badly, very badly. I was walking with this grandson of mine only this morning in the vineyard and it was always he who spotted the weeds—not me. Sit down, please, both of you, and I will bring you some food and wine."

"They are going to Osera to the Trappists."

"The Trappists are good men, but their wine, I believe, is less good and as for the liqueur they make. . . . You must take a case of wine for them and for yourselves too, of course. I've never had a monsignor here under my fig tree before."

"Sit down with them, Señor Diego," the young priest said, "and I will fetch the ham and the wine."

"The white and the red—and bowls for all of us. We will have a better feast than the Mexicans." When the priest was out of hearing he said, "If all the priests here were like my grandson. . . . I could trust him even with the vineyard. If only he had not chosen to be a priest. It was all his mother's fault. My son would never have allowed it. If he hadn't died. . . . I saw José today pulling up the weeds, but

I couldn't see them clearly any longer and I thought, 'It is time for me and the vineyard to go.' "

"Is this your grandson's parish?" Father Quixote asked.

"Oh no, no. He lives forty kilometers away. The priests here have driven him from his old parish. He was a danger to them. The poor people loved him because he refused to take money and say the Responses when anyone died. Responses, what nonsense! To gabble a few words and ask a thousand pesetas. So the priests wrote to the bishop and even though there were good Mexicans who defended him he was sent away. You would understand, if you stayed here a little while; you would see how greedy the priests are for the money the Mexicans have brought to these poor parts."

"Mexicans, Mexicans. But who are these Mexicans?"

The young priest came back to the fig tree carrying a tray with plates of ham, four large earthenware bowls and bottles of red and white wine. He filled the bowls with wine. "Start with the white," he said. "Make yourselves at home. Señor Diego and I had eaten before the Mexican arrived. Help yourselves to the ham—it is a good ham, home cured. You will not get such ham with the Trappists."

"But these Mexicans . . . please explain, father."

"Oh, they come here and build rich houses and the priests are corrupted by the sight of money. They even think they can buy Our Lady. Don't let's talk about them. There are better things to speak of."

"But who are these Mexicans . . . ?"

"Oh, there are good men among them. I don't deny it. Many good men, but all the same . . . I just don't understand. They have too much money and they have been away too long."

"Too long away from Mexico?"

"Too long away from Galicia. You are not taking any ham, monsignor. Please. . . ."

"I am very happy," Señor Diego said, "to welcome under this fig tree Monsignor . . . Monsignor . . ."

"Quixote," the Mayor said.

"Quixote? Not surely—"

"An unworthy descendant," Father Quixote interrupted him.

"And your friend?"

"As for myself," the Mayor said, "I cannot claim to be a true descendant of Sancho Panza. Sancho and I have a family name in common, that's all—but I can assure you that Monsignor Quixote and I have had some curious adventures. Even if they are not worthy to be compared. . . ."

"This is a very good wine," Señor Diego said, "but, José, go and fetch from the second barrel on the left . . . you know the one . . . only the very best is worthy of Monsignor Quixote and his friend Señor Sancho. And it is only in the best wine of all that we should toast damnation to the priests here."

When Father José had gone, Señor Diego added with a note of deep sadness, "I never expected a grandson of mine to be a priest." Father Quixote saw that there were tears in his eyes. "Oh, I am not running down the priesthood, monsignor, how could I do that? We have a good Pope, but what a suffering it must be at Mass every day, even for him, if he has to drink such bad wine as José's old priest buys."

"One takes the merest drop," Father Quixote said, "you hardly notice the taste. It's no worse than the wine that you get dolled up with a fancy label in a restaurant."

"Yes, you are quite right there, monsignor. Oh, every week there are scoundrels who come here to buy my wine so that they can mix it with other wine and they call it Rioja and advertise it along all the roads of Spain to deceive the poor foreigners who don't know a good wine from a bad."

"How can you tell the scoundrels from the honest men?"

"By the quantity they want to buy and because they often

don't even ask for a glass first to taste it." He added, "If only José had married and had had a son. I started teaching José about the vineyard when he was six years old and now he knows nearly as much as I do and his eyesight is so much better than mine. Soon he would have been teaching *his* son. . . ."

"Can't you find a good manager, Señor Diego?" the Mayor asked.

"That's a foolish question, Señor Sancho—one I would expect a Communist to ask."

"I am a Communist."

"Forgive me, I am not saying anything against Communists in their proper place, but their proper place is not a vineyard. You Communists could put managers in all the cement works of Spain if you liked. You could have managers over your brickworks and your armament firms, you could put them in charge of your gas and electricity, but you can't let them manage a vineyard."

"Why, Señor Diego?"

"A vine is alive like a flower or a bird. It is not something made by man—man can only help it to live—or to die," he added with a deep melancholy, so that his face lost all expression. He had shut his face, as a man shuts a book which he finds that he doesn't wish to read.

"Here is the best wine of all," Father José said—they had not heard him approach—and he began to pour into their bowls from a large jug.

"You are sure you took from the right barrel?" Señor Diego demanded.

"Of course I did. The second on the left."

"Then now we can drink damnation to the priests of these parts."

"Perhaps—I am really very thirsty—you would allow me to drink a little of this good wine before we decide on the toast?"

"Of course, monsignor. And let us have another toast first. To the Holy Father?"

"To the Holy Father and his intentions," Father Quixote said, making a slight amendment. "This is a truly magnificent wine, Señor Diego. I have to admit that our cooperative in El Toboso cannot produce its equal, though ours is an honest wine. But yours is more than honest—it is beautiful."

"I notice," Señor Diego said, "that your friend did not join in our toast. Surely even a Communist can toast the Holy Father's intentions?"

"Would you have toasted Stalin's intentions?" the Mayor demanded. "One can't know a man's intentions and one can't toast them. Do you think that the monsignor's ancestor really represented the chivalry of Spain? Oh, it may have been his intention, but we all make cruel parodies of what we intend." There was a note of sadness and regret in his voice which surprised Father Quixote. He had been accustomed to aggression from the Mayor—an aggression which was only perhaps a form of self-defense, but regret was surely a form of despair, of surrender, even perhaps of change. He thought for the first time: Where will this voyage of ours finally end?

Señor Diego said to his grandson, "Tell them who the Mexicans are. I thought all Spain knew of them."

"We haven't heard of them in El Toboso."

"The Mexicans," Father José said, "have come from Mexico, but they were all born here. They left Galicia to escape poverty, and escape it they did. They wanted money and they found money and they have come back to spend money. They give money to the priests here and they think they are giving to the Church. The priests have grown greedy for more—they prey on the poor and they prey on the superstition of the rich. They are worse than the Mexicans. Perhaps some of the Mexicans really believe they can buy their way into Heaven. But whose fault is that? Their priests know better and they sell Our Lady. You should see the feast they are celebrating in a town near here today. The priest puts Our Lady up to auction. The four Mexicans who pay the most will carry her in the procession."

"But this is unbelievable," Father Quixote exclaimed.

"Go and see for yourself."

Father Quixote put down his bowl. He said, "We must go, Sancho."

"The procession will not have started yet. Finish your wine first," Señor Diego urged him.

"I am sorry, Señor Diego, but I have lost my taste for even your best wine. You have told me my duty—'Go and see for yourself.' "

"What can you do, monsignor? Even the bishop supports them."

Father Quixote remembered the phrase he had used against his own bishop and he resisted the temptation to repeat it, though he was sorely tempted to use the words of his ancestor: "Under my cloak a fig for the king." "I thank you for your generous hospitality, Señor Diego," he said, "but I must go. Will you come with me, Sancho?"

"I would like to drink more of Señor Diego's wine, father, but I can't let you go alone."

"Perhaps in this affair it would be better if I went alone with Rocinante. I will come back for you. It is the honor of the Church which is concerned, so there is no reason for you—"

"Father, we have traveled the roads long enough together not to be parted now."

Señor Diego said, "José, put two cases of the best wine in their car. I shall always remember how under this fig tree I was able to entertain for a short while a descendant of the great Don."

2

They knew they were approaching the town when they began to pass many village folk on their way to the feast. It proved to be a very small town, hardly more than a village, and they could see the church, built on a hill, from far away. They passed a bank, the Banco Hispano Americano, which was closed like all the shops. "A big bank for so small a place," the Mayor commented, and a little farther down the road they passed five more. "Mexican money," the Mayor said.

"There are moments," Father Quixote replied, "when I am inclined to address you as *compañero*, but not yet, not yet."

"What do you propose to do, father?"

"I don't know. I am frightened, Sancho."

"Frightened of *them?*"

"No, no, frightened of myself."

"Why are you stopping?"

"Give me my *pechera*. It's behind you under the window. My collar too."

He got out of the car and a small group gathered in the street to watch him dress. He felt like an actor who is watched by friends in his dressing room.

"We are going into battle, Sancho. I need my armor. Even if it is as absurd as Mambrino's helmet."

He sat again behind the wheel of Rocinante and said, "I feel more ready now."

There must have been a hundred people waiting outside the church. Most of these were poor and they hung shyly back to give Father Quixote and Sancho better places near the entrance, where there was a group of men and women who were well-dressed—tradesmen perhaps or employees of the banks. As the poor separated to allow Father Quixote to pass, he asked one of them, "What is happening?"

"The auction is over, monsignor. They are fetching Our Lady from the church."

Another told him, "It went better than last year. You should have seen the money they paid."

"They started the auction at a thousand pesetas."

"The winner paid forty thousand."

"No, no, it was thirty."

"That was the second-best bid. You wouldn't think there was so much money in all Galicia."

"And the winner?" Father Quixote asked. "What does he win?"

One of the crowd laughed and spat on the ground. "Salvation for his sins. It's cheap at the price."

"Don't listen to him, monsignor. He laughs at all holy things. The winner—it's only fair—he has the best place among those who carry Our Lady. There is great competition."

"What is the best place?"

"In front on the right."

"Last year," the jester said, "there were only four bearers. The priest has made the stand bigger this year, so that there will be six."

"The last two paid only fifteen thousand."

"They had fewer sins to pay for. Next year, you will see, there will be eight bearers."

Father Quixote made his way nearer to the church door.

A man plucked his sleeve. He held out two fifty-peseta pieces. "Monsignor, would you give me a hundred-peseta note?"

"Why?"

"I want to give to Our Lady."

They were singing a hymn now in the church and Father Quixote could feel the tension and expectation in the crowd. He asked, "Won't Our Lady accept coins?"

Over their shoulders he could see the sway to and fro of 197 a crowned head, and he crossed himself in union with those around him. The coins slipped from the fingers of his neighbor who scrabbled on the ground to retrieve them. Between the heads of this man and that he got a glimpse of one of the bearers. It was the man with the striped tie. Then as the crowd retreated to make room the whole statue came for a moment into view.

Father Quixote could not understand what he saw. He was not offended by the customary image, with the plaster face, and the expressionless blue eyes, but the statue seemed to be clothed entirely in paper. A man pushed him to one side, waving a hundred-peseta note, and reached the statue. The carriers paused and gave him time to pin his note on the robes of the statue. It was impossible to see the robes for all the paper money—hundred-peseta notes, thousand-peseta notes, a five-hundred-franc note, and right over the heart a hundred-dollar bill. Between him and the statue there were only the priest and the fumes of the incense from his censer. Father Quixote gazed up at the crowned head and the glassy eyes which were like those of a woman dead and neglected—no one had bothered even to lower her lids. He thought: Was it for this she saw her son die in agony? To collect money? To make a priest rich?

The Mayor—he had quite forgotten that the Mayor was there behind him—said, "Come away, father."

"No, Sancho."

"Don't do anything foolish."

"Oh, you are talking like that other Sancho, and I say to you as my ancestor said when he saw the giants and you pretended they were windmills—'If you are afraid go away and say your prayers.' "

He took two steps forward and confronted the priest as he swung his censer to and fro. He said, "This is blasphemy."

The priest repeated, "Blasphemy?" Then he noticed Father Quixote's collar and his purple *pechera* and he added, "Monsignor."

"Yes. Blasphemy. If you know the meaning of the word."

"What do you mean, monsignor? This is our feast day. The feast day of our church. We have the blessing of the bishop."

"What bishop? No bishop would allow—"

The bearer with the extravagant tie interrupted. "The man is an impostor, father. I saw him earlier today. He wore no *pechera* then and no collar, and he was buying wine from that atheist Señor Diego."

"You have made your protest, father," the Mayor said. "Come away."

"Call the Guardia," the Mexican called to the crowd.

"You, you . . ." Father Quixote began, but the right word failed him in his anger. "Put down Our Lady. How dare you," he told the priest, "clothe her like that in money? It would be better to carry her through the streets naked."

"Fetch the Guardia," the Mexican repeated, but the situation was far too interesting for anyone in the crowd to stir.

The dissident called out, "Ask him where the money goes."

"For God's sake come away, father."

"Go on with the procession," the priest commanded.

"Over my dead body," Father Quixote said.

"Who are you? What right have you to interrupt our feast? What is your name?"

Father Quixote hesitated. He hated to use the title to which he felt he had no real claim. But his love for the woman whose image loomed above him conquered his reluctance. "I am Monsignor Quixote of El Toboso," he announced with firmness.

"It's a lie," the Mexican said.   199

"Lie or not, you have no authority in this diocese."

"I have the authority of any Catholic to fight blasphemy."

"Ask him where the money goes," the voice, which sounded too arrogant in his ears, called again from the crowd, but one cannot always choose one's allies.

Father Quixote took a step forward.

"That's right. Hit him. He's only a priest. This is a republic now."

"Call the Guardia. The man's a Communist." It was the Mexican who spoke.

The priest tried to swing his censer between the statue and Father Quixote as though he expected that the smoke might hold him back, and the censer struck Father Quixote on the side of his head. A trickle of blood curved round his right eye.

"Father, we've got to go," the Mayor urged him.

Father Quixote thrust the priest aside. He pulled the hundred-dollar bill off the statue's robe, tearing the robe and the bill. There was a five-hundred-franc note pinned on the other side. This one came away easily and he let it drop. Several hundred-peseta notes were split in pieces when he snatched at them. He rolled them into a ball and tossed it away into the crowd. The dissident cheered and there were three or four voices which joined him. The Mexican lowered the pole of the statue's stand which he was supporting and the whole affair reeled sideways so that Our Lady's crown tipped drunkenly over her left eye. The weight was too much for another Mexican, who let go his pole and Our Lady went crashing to the earth. It was like the end of an orgy. The dissident led a group forward to salvage some of the notes and there was a confused struggle with the bearers.

The Mayor grasped Father Quixote by the shoulder and pushed him out of the way. Only the Mexican with the tie noticed and screamed above the noise of the fray, "Thief!

Blasphemer! Impostor!" He took a deep breath and added, "Communist!"

"You've done quite enough for today," the Mayor said.

"Where are you taking me? Forgive me. I am confused. . . ." Father Quixote put his hand to his head and took it away blood-stained. "Did somebody hit me?"

"You can't start a revolution without bloodshed."

"I didn't really mean. . . ." In his confusion he allowed the Mayor to lead him away to the place where Rocinante waited. "I feel a little giddy," he said. "I don't know why."

The Mayor looked back. He saw that the Mexican had detached himself from the fight and was talking to the priest, flailing his arms.

"Get in quick," the Mayor said, "we have to be off."

"Not that seat. I have to drive Rocinante."

"You can't drive. You are a casualty."

"But she doesn't like a strange hand."

"My hands are no longer strange to her. Didn't I drive her all the way back to rescue you?"

"Please don't overstrain her. She's old."

"She's young enough to do a hundred."

Father Quixote gave way without further protest. He sank back in his seat as far as Rocinante permitted. Anger had always exhausted him—and even more the thoughts which were liable to come after. "Oh dear, oh dear," he said, "whatever will the bishop say if he hears?"

"He certainly will hear, but what worries me is what the Guardia will say—and do."

The needle on the speedometer approached a hundred.

"Causing a riot. That's the most serious crime you've committed so far. We have to find sanctuary." The Mayor added, "I would have preferred Portugal, but the monastery of Osera is better than nothing."

They had driven in silence for more than half an hour before the Mayor spoke again. "Are you asleep?"

201

"No."

"It's not like you to be so silent."

"I am suffering from one indisputable aspect of the Natural Law. I very much want to relieve myself."

"Can't you hold on for another half hour? We should be at the monastery by then."

"I'm afraid I can't."

Unwillingly the Mayor brought Rocinante to a halt beside a field and what looked like an ancient Celtic cross. While Father Quixote emptied his bladder the Mayor read the inscription which was nearly worn away.

"That's better. I feel able to talk again now," Father Quixote told him, when he returned.

"It's very odd," the Mayor said. "Did you notice that old cross in the field?"

"Yes."

"It's not as old as you might think. 1928 is the date and it's been put up in that field far from anywhere in memory of a school inspector. Why there? Why a school inspector?"

"Perhaps he was killed at that spot. A motor accident?"

"Or perhaps the Guardia," the Mayor said with a glance in his mirror, but the road was empty behind them.

IV

HOW MONSIGNOR QUIXOTE REJOINED HIS ANCESTOR

The great gray edifice of the Osera monastery stretches out almost alone within a trough of the Galician hills. A small shop and a bar at the very entrance of the monastery grounds make up the whole village of Osera. The carved exterior which dates from the sixteenth century hides the twelfth-century interior—an imposing stairway, perhaps twenty meters wide, up which a platoon could march shoulder to shoulder, leads to long passages lined with guest rooms above the central courtyard and the cloisters. Almost the only sound during the day is the ring of hammers where half a dozen workmen are struggling to repair the ravages of seven centuries. Sometimes a white-robed figure passes rapidly by on what is apparently a serious errand, and in dark corners loom the wooden figures of popes and of the knights whose order founded the monastery. They take on an appearance of life, as sad memories do, when the dark has fallen. A visitor has the impression of an abandoned island which has been colonized only recently by a small group of adventurers, who are now trying to make a home in the ruins of a past civilization.

The doors of the church, which open onto the little square before the monastery, are closed except during visiting hours and at the time of Sunday Masses, but the monks have their private staircase which leads from the corridor, where the guest rooms lie, down to the great nave as large as many a cathedral's. Only during visiting hours or when guests are present do human voices sound among the ancient stones, as though a pleasure boat has deposited a few tourists on the shore.

2

Father Leopoldo was only too well aware that he had cooked a very bad lunch for the guest room. He had no illusions about his ability as a chef, but his fellow Trappists were used to even worse cooking and there was no real occasion for them to complain—each of them in turn would have to do his best or his worst. All the same, most guests must have been accustomed to better food, and Father Leopoldo felt unhappy when he thought of the meal he had served that afternoon, all the more because he had a real reverence for the only guest at the moment, who was the Professor of Hispanic Studies at Notre Dame University in the United States. Professor Pilbeam had taken—it would appear from the plate—not more than a spoonful or two of soup, and his fish had been left almost untouched. The lay brother who was helping Father Leopoldo in the kitchen had raised his eyebrows ostentatiously when the professor's dishes were brought in to be cleaned and he had winked at Father Leopoldo. When there is a vow of silence, a wink can convey as much as a word, and no one there had taken a vow to refrain from communication by other means than the voice.

Father Leopoldo was glad when at last he was able to leave the kitchen and go to the library. He hoped that he would find the professor there, for then he could tell him in words how sorry he was about the meals. Speech was not forbidden with a guest, and he felt sure that Professor Pilbeam would understand his absent-mindedness with the salt. He had been thinking, as happened very often, of Descartes. The presence of Professor Pilbeam, whose second visit to Osera this was, had removed Father Leopoldo from the peace of a routine to a more confused world, the world of intellectual speculation. Professor Pilbeam was perhaps the greatest living authority on the life and works of Ignatius Loyola, and any intellectual discussion, even on a subject as unsympathetic to Father Leopoldo as a Jesuit saint, was like giving food to a starving man. It could be dangerous. So often the guests at the monastery were young people of great piety who imagined that they had a vocation for a Trappist life, and they invariably irritated him by their ignorance and by their exaggerated respect for what they believed had been his great sacrifice. They wanted in a romantic way to sacrifice their own lives. But he had come here only to find a precarious peace.

The professor was not in the library and Father Leopoldo sat down and again he thought of Descartes. It was Descartes who had led him out of skepticism into the Church in much the same way as he had led the Queen of Sweden. Descartes would certainly not have put too much salt in the soup, nor would he have overgrilled the fish. Descartes was a practical man who had worked on spectacles to find cures for blindness and on wheelchairs to aid cripples. Father Leopoldo when a young man had no thought of becoming a priest. He had attached himself to Descartes without thought of where he might be led. He wanted to question everything, in the manner of Descartes, searching for an absolute truth, and in the end, like Descartes, he had accepted what seemed to him the nearest thing to truth. But it was then that he had taken a greater leap than Descartes—a leap into the silent world of Osera. He was not unhappy—except about the soup and the fish—but all the same he was glad of the opportunity to talk to an intelligent man, even if he had to talk about Saint Ignatius rather than Descartes.

After a while, when there was no sign of Professor Pilbeam, he made his way along the guests' corridor and down to the great church which was likely to be empty at this hour when the outer doors were closed. There were few, except during tourist hours, who visited the church—even on a Sunday—so that to Father Leopoldo it was like a close family home, almost free from the intrusion of strangers. There he could pray his individual prayer, and it was there he would often pray for Descartes, and sometimes he would even pray to Descartes. The church was ill-lit, and as he entered by the private door from the monastery he did not at first recognize a figure which stood examining the rather grotesque painting of a naked man stuck in a thorn bush. Then the man spoke in his American accent—it was Professor Pilbeam.

"I know you are not very fond of Saint Ignatius," he said, "but at least he was a good soldier and a good soldier would find more useful ways of suffering than throwing himself into a lot of thorns."

Father Leopoldo abandoned the thought of private prayer, and in any case the rare opportunity to speak was a greater privilege. He said, "I am not so sure that Saint Ignatius was all that concerned with what was useful. A soldier can be very romantic. I think it is for that reason he is a national hero. All Spaniards are romantic, so that sometimes we take windmills for giants."

"Windmills?"

"You know that one of our great modern philosophers compared Saint Ignatius to Don Quixote. They had a lot in common."

"I haven't read Cervantes since I was a boy. Too fanciful

for my taste. I haven't much time for fiction. Facts are what I like. If I could unearth one undiscovered document about Saint Ignatius I would die a happy man."

"Fact and fiction—they are not always easy to distinguish. As you are a Catholic. . . ."

"A rather nominal one, father, I'm afraid. I haven't bothered to change the label that I was born with. And of course being a Catholic helps me in my research—it opens doors. Now you, Father Leopoldo, you are a student of Descartes. That's hardly likely to open many doors for you, I should imagine. What brought you here?"

"I suppose Descartes brought me to the point where he brought himself—to faith. Fact or fiction—in the end you can't distinguish between them—you just have to choose."

"But to become a Trappist?"

"I think, you know, professor, that when one has to jump, it's so much safer to jump into deep water."

"And you don't regret . . . ?"

"Professor, there are always plenty of things to regret. Regrets are part of life. One can't escape regrets even in a twelfth-century monastery. Can you escape from them in the University of Notre Dame?"

"No, but I decided long ago that I was not a jumper."

It was an unfortunate remark, for at that moment jump he did as an explosion outside was followed seconds later by two more, and the sound of a crash.

"A tire gone," Professor Pilbeam exclaimed. "I'm afraid there's been a motor accident."

"That was no tire," Father Leopoldo said. "Those were gunshots." He made for the stairs and called back over his shoulder, "The church doors are locked. Follow me." He ran down the passage by the guest rooms as fast as his long robe would allow him and arrived out of breath at the head of the great ceremonial staircase. The professor was close behind. "Go and find Father Enrique. Tell him to open the church doors. If someone's been hurt we can't carry him up all these stairs."

Father Francisco, who was in charge of the little shop near the entrance, had left his picture postcards, rosaries and liqueur bottles. He looked frightened, and scrupulously he waved his hand towards the door without breaking his vow of silence.

A small Seat car had smashed against the wall of the church. Two Guardia had left their jeep and were approaching with caution with their guns at the ready. A man with blood on his face was trying to open the door of the Seat. He called angrily to the Guardia, "Come and help, you assassins. We are not armed."

Father Leopoldo said, "Are you hurt?"

"Of course I'm hurt. That's nothing. I think they've killed my friend."

The Guardia put away their guns. One of them said, "We only shot at the tires." The other explained, "We had our orders. These men were wanted for causing a riot."

Father Leopoldo looked at the passenger through the shattered glass of the windscreen. He exclaimed, "But he's a priest," and a moment later, "a monsignor."

"Yes," the stranger said with anger, "a monsignor—and if the monsignor hadn't stopped to piss we would have been safe in your monastery by now."

The two Guardia managed to wrench the passenger door open. "He's alive," one of them said.

"No thanks to you."

"You are both under arrest. Get into the jeep while we pull your friend out."

The doors of the church swung open and Professor Pilbeam joined them.

Father Leopoldo said, "These men are injured. You can't take them away like this."

"They are wanted for causing a riot and stealing money."

"Nonsense. The man in the car is a monsignor. Monsignors don't steal money. What's your friend's name?" he asked the stranger.

"Monsignor Quixote."

"Quixote! Impossible," Professor Pilbeam said.

"Monsignor Quixote of El Toboso. A descendant of the great Don Quixote himself."

"Don Quixote had no descendants. How could he? He's a fictional character."

"Fact and fiction again, professor. So difficult to distinguish," Father Leopoldo said.

The Guardia had succeeded in removing Father Quixote from the wrecked car and they laid him on the ground. He was trying to speak. The stranger leaned over him. "If he dies," he told the Guardia, "by God, I'll see you pay for this."

One of the Guardia looked uneasy, but the other demanded sharply, "What is your name?"

"Zancas, Enrique, but monsignor," he rolled the title as though it were a salute or a drum, "prefers to call me Sancho."

"Profession?"

"I am the former Mayor of El Toboso."

"Your papers."

"You are welcome to them if you can find them in this wreck."

"Señor Zancas," Father Leopoldo said, "can you make out what the monsignor is trying to say?"

"He is asking if Rocinante is all right."

"Rocinante!" Professor Pilbeam exclaimed. "But Rocinante was a horse."

"He means the car. I daren't tell him. The shock might be too great."

"Professor, will you please telephone to Orense for a doctor? Father Francisco knows the number."

The surly Guardia said, "We can see about the doctor. We are taking them to Orense."

"Not in this condition. I forbid it."

"We will have an ambulance sent."

"You can send your ambulance if you want, but it may have to wait a long time: these two will stay here in the monastery until the doctor allows them to leave. I shall speak to the bishop in Orense and I am sure he will have something to say to your commanding officer. Now don't you dare to finger your gun at me."

"We'll go and report," the other Guardia said.

Professor Pilbeam returned with a monk. They carried a mattress between them. He said, "Father Francisco is telephoning. This will have to do for a stretcher."

Father Quixote was shifted with some difficulty onto the mattress and the four of them carried him into the church and up the nave. He was muttering what might have been prayers, but might equally well have been curses. As they turned in front of the altar towards the stairs he made an attempt to cross himself, but the cross remained uncompleted. He had fainted again. The stairs were a difficulty and they had to take a rest at the top.

Professor Pilbeam said, "Quixote is not a Spanish family name. Cervantes himself said that the real name was probably Quexana and his home was not in El Toboso."

The Mayor said, "Nor was Monsignor Quixote born there."

"Where was he born?"

The Mayor quoted, " 'In a certain village in La Mancha which I do not wish to name.' "

"But the whole story is absurd. And Rocinante. . . ."

Father Leopoldo said, "Let us put him safely to bed in number three guest room before we discuss the difficult distinction between fact and fiction."

Father Quixote opened his eyes. "Where am I?" he asked. "I thought . . . I thought . . . I was in a church."

"You were, monsignor. The church of Osera. Now we are taking you to a guest room where you can sleep comfortably till the doctor comes."

"Again a doctor. Oh dear, oh dear, is my health so bad . . . ?"

"A little rest, and you will be yourself again."

"I thought . . . in the church . . . and then there were some stairs . . . I thought if I could only say a Mass. . . ."

"Perhaps . . . tomorrow . . . when you are rested."

"Too long since I said one. Sick . . . traveling. . . ."

"Don't worry, monsignor. Perhaps tomorrow."

They got him safely into his room and presently the doctor from Orense came and told them he thought there was nothing seriously wrong—shock and a minor cut on his forehead from the broken windscreen. Of course at his age. . . . Tomorrow he would examine him more thoroughly. Perhaps an X-ray might be necessary. Meanwhile he should be kept quiet. It was the Mayor who needed more attention, more attention in more than one way because after the doctor had finished with him (a half dozen or so stitches) the head of the Guardia in Orense telephoned. The Guardia had checked up on Father Quixote by telephone to La Mancha—his bishop there had told them that he was in fact a monsignor (by some oversight of the Holy Father), but his mental health made him irresponsible for his actions. As for his companion—that was quite another matter. It was true that he had been mayor of El Toboso, but he had been defeated at the last election and he was a notorious Communist.

Luckily it was Father Leopoldo who answered the telephone. He said, "At Osera we are not concerned with a man's politics. He will stay here until he is fit to travel."

•

3

The doctor had given Father Quixote a sedative. He slept deeply and it was one o'clock in the morning before he woke. He couldn't make out where he was. He called, "Teresa," but there was no reply. Somewhere there were voices —male voices—and an idea came to him that Father Herrera and the bishop were discussing him in the sitting room. He got out of his bed, but his legs folded under him and he sank down again and cried out more urgently for Teresa.

The Mayor came in, closely followed by Father Leopoldo. Professor Pilbeam watched from the door without entering. "Are you in pain, monsignor?" Father Leopoldo asked.

"Please do not call me monsignor, Doctor Galván. I have no right even to say Mass. The bishop forbids it. He would even like to burn my books."

"What books?"

"The books I love. Saint Francis de Sales, Saint Augustine, Señorita Martin of Lisieux. I don't think he trusts me even with Saint John." He put his hand to the bandage on his head. "I am glad to be back in El Toboso. But perhaps at this very moment Father Herrera is burning my books outside."

"Don't worry. In a day or two—father—you will feel yourself again. For the moment you must rest."

"It's difficult to rest, doctor. There is so much in my head that wants to come out. Your white coat—you are not going to operate, are you?"

"Of course not," Father Leopoldo reassured him, "just another pill to make you sleep."

"Why, Sancho, is that you? I'm glad to see you. You found your way home all right. How is Rocinante?"

"Very tired. She's resting in the garage."

"What an old pair we are. I am tired too."

Without resistance he took the pill and almost immediately fell asleep.

"I'll sit up with him," Sancho said.

"I'll stay with you. I wouldn't be able to sleep for worrying," Father Leopoldo said.

"I'll lie down for a while," Professor Pilbeam told them. "You know my room. Wake me if I can be of any use."

It was around three in the morning when Father Quixote spoke and awoke the two of them from a shallow drowse. He said, "Excellency, a lamb may be able to tame an elephant, but I would beg you to remember the goats in your prayers."

"Dreaming or delirium?" Father Leopoldo wondered.

Sancho said, "I seem to remember. . . ."

"You have no right to burn my books, Excellency. The sword, I beg you, not death by pin stabs."

There was a short period of silence, then, "A fart," Father Quixote said, "can be musical."

"I fear," Father Leopoldo whispered, "that he is in a worse state than the doctor told us."

"Mambrino," came the voice from the bed, "Mambrino's helmet. Give it me."

"What does 'Mambrino's helmet' mean?"

Sancho said, "It was the barber's basin which Don Quixote wore. His ancestor, as he believes."

"The professor seems to regard all that as nonsense."

"So does the bishop, which inclines me to think that it may be true."

"I am sorry and beg pardon for the half bottle. It was a sin against the Holy Ghost."

"What does he mean by that?"

"It would take too long to explain now."

"Man has learned many important things from the beasts: from storks the enema, from elephants chastity, and loyalty from the horse."

213

"That sounds like Saint Francis de Sales," Father Leopoldo whispered.

"No. I think it is Cervantes," Professor Pilbeam corrected them as he entered the room.

For a while there was silence. "He sleeps again," Father Leopoldo whispered. "Perhaps he will be more peaceful when he wakes."

"Silence with him is not always a sign of peace," Sancho said. "It sometimes means an agony of spirit."

The voice that came from the bed, however, sounded strong and firm. "I don't offer you a governorship, Sancho. I offer you a kingdom."

"Speak to him," Father Leopoldo urged.

"A kingdom?" Sancho repeated.

"Come with me, and you will find the kingdom."

"I will never leave you, father. We have been on the road together too long for that."

"By this hopping you can recognize love."

Father Quixote sat up on the bed and threw off the sheets. "You condemn me, Excellency, not to say my Mass even in private. That is a shameful thing. For I am innocent. I repeat openly to you the words I used to Doctor Galván—'Bugger the bishop.'" He put his feet to the ground, staggered for a moment and stood firm. "By this hopping," he repeated, "you can recognize love."

He walked to the door of the room and fumbled for a moment with the handle. He turned and looked through the three of them as though they were made of glass. "No balloons," he remarked in a note of deep sadness, "no balloons."

"Follow him," Father Leopoldo told the Mayor.

"Shouldn't we wake him?"

"No. It might be dangerous. Let him play out his dream."

Father Quixote walked slowly and carefully out into the
passage and moved towards the great staircase, but perhaps

some memory of the route by which they had carried him from the church made him pause. He addressed one of the wooden painted figures—pope or knight?—and asked quite lucidly, "Is this the way to your church?" He seemed to receive an answer, for he turned on his heel and passed Sancho without a word, going this time in the right direction for the private stair. They followed him cautiously so as not to disturb him.

"Suppose he falls on the stairs," the Mayor whispered.

"To wake him would be even more dangerous."

Father Quixote led them down into the shadows of the great church lit only by the half moon which shone through the east window. He walked firmly to the altar and began to say the words of the old Latin Mass, but it was in an oddly truncated form. He began with the response, "*Et introibo ad altare Dei, qui laetificat juventutem meam.*"

"Is he conscious of what he is doing?" Professor Pilbeam whispered.

"God knows," Father Leopoldo answered.

The Mass went rapidly on—no epistle, no gospel: it was as though Father Quixote were racing towards the consecration. Because he feared interruption from the bishop? the Mayor wondered. From the Guardia? Even the long list of saints from Peter to Damien was omitted.

"When he finds no paten and no chalice, surely he will wake," Father Leopoldo said. The Mayor moved a few steps nearer to the altar. He was afraid that, when the moment of waking came, Father Quixote might fall, and he wanted to be near enough to catch him in his arms.

"Who the day before He suffered took bread. . . ." Father Quixote seemed totally unaware that there was no Host, no paten waiting on the altar. He raised empty hands, "*Hoc est enim corpus meum,*" and afterwards he went steadily on without hesitation to the consecration of the non-existent wine in the non-existent chalice.   215

Father Leopoldo and the professor had knelt from custom at the words of consecration: the Mayor remained standing. He wanted to be prepared if Father Quixote faltered.

"*Hic est enim calix sanguinis mei.*" The empty hands seemed to be fashioning a chalice out of the air.

"Sleep? Delirium? Madness?" Professor Pilbeam whispered the question. The Mayor edged his way a few more steps towards the altar. He was afraid to distract Father Quixote. As long as he was speaking the Latin words he was at least happy in his dream. In the years which had passed since his youth at Salamanca the Mayor had forgotten most of the Mass. What remained in his head were certain key passages which had appealed to him emotionally at that distant time. Father Quixote seemed to be suffering from the same lapse of memory—perhaps in all the years of saying the Mass, almost mechanically, by heart, it was only those sentences, which like the nightlights of childhood had lit the dark room of habit, that he was recalling now.

So it was he remembered the Our Father, and from there his memory leapt to the *Agnus Dei*. "*Agnus Dei qui tollis peccata mundi.*" He paused and shook his head. For a moment the Mayor thought he was waking from his dream. He whispered so softly that only the Mayor caught his words, "Lamb of God, but the goats, the goats," then he went directly on to the prayer of the Roman centurion: "Lord, I am not worthy that Thou shouldst enter under my roof; say but the word and my soul shall be healed."

His Communion was approaching. The professor said, "Surely when he finds nothing there to take, he will wake up."

"I wonder," Father Leopoldo replied. He added, "I wonder if he will ever wake again."

216   For a few seconds Father Quixote remained silent. He

swayed a little back and forth before the altar. The Mayor took another step forward, ready to catch him, but then he spoke again: "*Corpus Domini nostri*," and with no hesitation at all he took from the invisible paten the invisible Host and his fingers laid the nothing on his tongue. Then he raised the invisible chalice and seemed to drink from it. The Mayor could see the movement of his throat as he swallowed.

For the first time he appeared to become conscious that he was not alone in the church. He looked around him with a puzzled air. Perhaps he was seeking the communicants. He remarked the Mayor standing a few feet from him and took the non-existent Host between his fingers; he frowned as though something mystified him and then he smiled. "*Compañero*," he said, "you must kneel, *compañero.*" He came forward three steps with two fingers extended, and the Mayor knelt. Anything which will give him peace, he thought, anything at all. The fingers came closer. The Mayor opened his mouth and felt the fingers, like a Host, on his tongue. "By this hopping," Father Quixote said, "by this hopping," and then his legs gave way. The Mayor had only just time to catch him and ease him to the ground. "*Compañero*," the Mayor repeated the word in his turn, "this is Sancho," and he felt over and over again without success for the beat of Father Quixote's heart.

4

The guest master—a very old man called Father Felipe— told the Mayor that he thought he might find Father Leopoldo in the library. It was visiting hour and Father Felipe was leading a straggling group of tourists around the parts of the monastery open to the public. There were elderly ladies who listened to every word with what seemed deep respect, some obvious husbands who by their detached air deliberately communicated the fact that they were only following the procession to please their wives, and three youths who had to be restrained from smoking—they were obviously crestfallen because the two pretty girls in the party showed not the least interest in their presence. Their masculinity seemed to have no appeal to the girls, but the celibacy and the silence in the old building were like a provocative perfume and they gazed with fascination at the notice *"Claustura"* which at one point stopped their progress like a traffic sign, as though beyond it there might be secrets more interesting and perverse than anything the young men could offer.

One young man tried a door and found it locked. To draw attention to himself he called, "Hi, father, what's in here?"

"One of our guests who is sleeping late," Father Felipe replied.

A very long and very late sleep, the Mayor thought. It was the room where the body of Father Quixote lay. He stood and watched the party as it passed down the long corridor of guest rooms and then he turned towards the library. There he found the professor and Father Leopoldo walking up and down. "Fact and fiction again," Father Leopoldo was saying, "one can't distinguish with any certainty."

The Mayor said, "I have come, father, to say goodbye."

"You are very welcome to stay here awhile."

"I suppose Father Quixote's body will be taken off to El Toboso today. I think I would do better in Portugal where I have friends. If you would allow me to use the telephone for a taxi to Orense where I can hire a car?"

The professor said, "I will drive you in. I have to go to Orense myself."

"You don't want to attend Father Quixote's funeral?" Father Leopoldo asked the Mayor.

218

"What one does with the body is not very important, is it?"

"A very Christian thought," Father Leopoldo remarked.

"Besides," the Mayor said, "I think my being there would disturb the bishop, who will certainly be present if he is to be buried in El Toboso."

"Ah yes, the bishop. He has been on the telephone already this morning. He wanted me to tell the abbot to make quite sure that Father Quixote would not be allowed to say Mass even in private. I explained the sad circumstances which made it quite certain that his order would be obeyed —in future, that is."

"What did he say?"

"Nothing, but I thought I heard a sigh of relief."

"Why did you say 'in future'? What we listened to last night could hardly be described as a Mass," the professor said.

"Are you sure of that?" Father Leopoldo asked.

"Of course I am. There was no consecration."

"I repeat—are you sure?"

"Of course I'm sure. There was no Host and no wine."

"Descartes, I think, would have said rather more cautiously than you that he *saw* no bread or wine."

"You know as well as I do that there *was* no bread and no wine."

"I know as well as you—or as little—yes, I agree to that. But Monsignor Quixote quite obviously believed in the presence of the bread and wine. Which of us was right?"

"We were."

"Very difficult to prove that logically, professor. Very difficult indeed."

"You mean," the Mayor asked, "that I may have received Communion?"

"You certainly did—in *his* mind. Does it matter to you?"

"To me, no. But I'm afraid in the eyes of your Church I'm a very unworthy recipient. I am a Communist. One 219 who has not been to confession for thirty years or more. What I've done in those thirty years—well, you wouldn't like me to go into details."

"Perhaps Monsignor Quixote knew your state of mind better than you do yourself. You have been friends. You have traveled together. He encouraged you to take the Host. He showed no hesitation. I distinctly heard him say, 'Kneel, *compañero.*' "

"There was no Host," the professor persisted in a tone of deep irritation, "whatever Descartes might have said. You are arguing for the sake of arguing. You are misusing Descartes."

"Do you think it's more difficult to turn empty air into wine than wine into blood? Can our limited senses decide a thing like that? We are faced by an infinite mystery."

The Mayor said, "I prefer to think there was no Host."

"Why?"

"Because once when I was young I partly believed in a God, and a little of that superstition still remains. I'm rather afraid of mystery, and I am too old to change my spots. I prefer Marx to mystery, father."

"You were a good friend and you are a good man. You don't want my blessing, but you will have to accept it all the same. Don't be embarrassed. It's just a habit we have, like sending cards at Christmas."

While the Mayor waited for the professor he bought a small bottle of liqueur and two picture postcards from Father Felipe because they had refused to take money for lodging him or even for the telephone call. He didn't want to be grateful—gratitude was like a handcuff which only the captor could release. He wanted to feel free, but he had the sense that somewhere on the road from El Toboso he had lost his freedom. It's only human to doubt, Father Quixote had told him, but to doubt, he thought, is to lose the freedom of action. Doubting, one begins to waver between one action and another. It was not by doubting that Newton discovered the law of gravity or Marx the future of capitalism.

He went over to the wrecked carcass of Rocinante. He felt glad that Father Quixote had not seen her in that state, half on her side against the wall, the windscreen in smithereens, one door wrenched off its hinges, the other caved in, her tyres flattened by the bullets of the Guardia: there was no more of a future for Rocinante than for Father Quixote. They had died within a few hours of each other —a broken mass of metal, a brain in fragments. He insisted with a kind of ferocity on the likeness, fighting for a certainty: that the human being is also a machine. But Father Quixote had felt love for this machine.

A horn sounded and he turned his back on Rocinante to join Professor Pilbeam. As he took his seat the professor said, "Father Leopoldo is a little absurd about Descartes. I suppose in that silence, which they all have to keep here, strange ideas get nourished like mushrooms in a dark cellar."

"Yes. Perhaps."

The Mayor didn't speak again before they reached Orense; an idea quite strange to him had lodged in his brain. Why is it that the hate of a man—even of a man like Franco—dies with his death, and yet love, the love which he had begun to feel for Father Quixote, seemed now to live and grow in spite of the final separation and the final silence—for how long, he wondered with a kind of fear, was it possible for that love of his to continue? And to what end?